Once Upon a Time
a Time
BY THE
LINESIDE

by
Ken Jones

CHALLENGER U.K.

First published in the United Kingdom
by CHALLENGER U.K. 1998
ISBN 1 899624 11 2
Copyright Challenger U.K. & K.G.Jones

The CAPITALS UNITED EXPRESS billed between Paddington and Cardiff, actually ventured as far as Neyland. In this photograph "Britannia" Pacific 70027 RISING STAR, allocated to Cardiff Canton, races under Dog Kennel bridge, west of Iver, on a Spring Saturday in 1960. In 1957 Cardiff's allocation of "Britannia" locomotives totalled fifteen, but by closure of Canton in 1962 all had been transferred away to Midland depots, although prior to this some transfers within the Western Region had taken place. The 86C shed plate on the locomotive dates the scene prior to October 1960, since on that date Cardiff Canton was recoded 88A.

CHALLENGER U.K.
309 Mapperley Plains, Nottingham, NG3 5RG
Printed and bound by
The Amadeus Press, Huddersfield

Once Upon a Time by the Lineside

Contents

Introduction..1

1. Western Region Tour 1960 - Rover Ticket Style.......7

2. No Loitering at Iver Station Please........................17

3. Paddington, Old Oak and Southall.......................27

4. Down the Main to Reading...................................37

5. From Reading to Didcot and Oxford.....................45

6. Swindon Factory - Last Breath of Steam................55

7. Sojourn to Bristol...63

8. South Wales - The Land of the Red Dragon............71

9. North to Shrewsbury via the GW/GC Joint............81

10. Days on the Southern..91

Cover illustrations

Front cover:-
(top) **"Hall" 6997 speeds through Iver with a Down semi-fast, 24th August 1963.**

(middle) **"O2" 0-4-4T No.20 waits to depart Ryde Pier station with a service to Ventnor, 14th August 1965.**

(bottom) **Type 3 diesel-electric D6545 takes the Chertsey line at Weybridge with a goods train, made up mainly of mineral wagons, in August 1966.**

Rear cover:-
(top) **"King" Class 6015 KING RICHARD III is working hard through Iver with the 9.15 a.m. Paddington to Durston early in 1960.**

(bottom) **Without doubt the best loved tank engines on the Southern were the diminutive "Terriers". They were the mainstay of the Hayling Island branch service from Havant until the closure of the line from 3rd November 1963. After replenishing its tanks with water and running round its train, 32650 has attached to a three carriage make-up and half obscured by steam, makes a hasty departure from Langstone for Havant. Having sought permission I ventured onto the track to take this pleasing scene. The last day, this would never be seen again.**

INTRODUCTION

I could never attempt to explain the magnetic attraction of steam that drew me to the lineside during the 1950's and 60's for hours of endless observations. Only fellow enthusiasts of the time will understand, proven by the vast number of books, magazine articles and video taped film produced by enthusiasts for the enjoyment of everyone interested in railways as a pastime. This recorded material fosters the nostalgic elements belonging to the steam era and to some extent the early days of the diesels, particularly the Western Region hydraulics, many of which perpetuated the Great Western tradition of carrying names.

The variety of locomotive types and the apparent large number of examples in each class encouraged the collecting instinct in the younger generation of the time; I was no exception. Once hooked it was difficult, if not impossible, to lose interest. It seemed that collecting the numbers of steam engines was an added bonus to merely watching those magnificent man-made beasts beat the staccato rhythm of rail joints and steam exhaust. Within a very short space of time I was introduced to the *WESTERN REGION ABC* book, which set the target of seeing every engine recorded in Western Region stock.

My home patch was the Western Region main line out of Paddington and by 1962 most of the ex-GW locomotives had been underlined (as seen) in my ABC book, although after 1960 new sightings were invariably at other locations on the region where tank engines roamed the lesser byways of the system.

My efforts at seeing every engines gathered momentum following the introduction of diesels, but the pace of modernisation and the consequent rate of steam engine scrapping made this task impossible. Nevertheless I had seen 97% of the book stock by the end of Western steam (based on the 1958 ABC). However, this wasn't quite the end as three of the unseen engines were discovered in the steam graveyard at Barry Docks ten years later.

Following the creation of a record of observations on a rail-rover trip of the Western Region in 1960, I realised that everything being observed was quickly going to disappear with advancing modernisation. Thus started a series of notebook records with a gathering interest in photography which has lasted to this day. It is from these records, photographs and some earlier memories that is drawn the material for this book.

The very first seed of railway interest was sown on a junior school trip to the Festival of Britain in 1951. On exhibition was the new design of Standard British Railways express locomotive "Britannia" Class 70004 WILLIAM SHAKESPEARE. Two years were to pass before the seed blossomed into full blown railway mania.

On my inaugural visit to the lineside at Iver in 1953 the first locomotive I remember seeing was "6100" Class tank 6154 with a suburban train to Slough. Very soon after I had recorded "Castle" Class 5050 EARL OF ST. GERMANS, very rarely seen in the London division at that time, being allocated to Shrewsbury (84G): No one believed me!

Everyone had favourite engines which despite being commonly seen were enthusiastically tolerated compared to the regular sighting of some "Modified Halls" with unimpressive names and grimy appearances, at least I thought that at the time. Of my favourites 4037 THE SOUTH WALES BORDERERS, 5091 CLEEVE ABBEY and 7823 HOOK NORTON MANOR are high on the list.

On the 20th November, 1955 disaster struck. My favourite "Britannia" 70026 POLAR STAR suffered a serious accident at Milton, near Didcot, hauling an excursion train from Treherbert to Paddington. The train was diverted to the up goods loop and the excessive speed of 70026 over the curved facing crossover caused the engine to derail, career off the track and tumble down an embankment killing eleven people and causing injury to many more.

I later saw the engine at Swindon, very much mangled, with a gaping hole in the tender.

One could be forgiven for believing that my sole interest lay in those brass numbered brunswick green Great Western locomotives, and the Western based "Britannia" Pacifics, but it is natural that a primary allegiance should fall with the locomotives pounding the beat of ones home territory.

Travel whilst at school, with limited funds, was naturally restricted to cycle trips to local lines and visits to the lineside while on holiday. A Christmas present of a racing style cycle gave me the spirit to venture further afield and later with an 800 c.c. Morris Minor, which laboured at speeds in excess of 50 m.p.h., my field of observation widened further.

When I think of the destinations achieved by pedal power I wonder how I mustered the energy. Regularly, when the weather was favourable, my drop handled bar "Rocket" took me to Old Oak Common, Willesden, Neadsden and Cricklewood depots, as well as lineside visits to Northwick Park (Euston main line), Wood Green (Kings Cross main line), St. Albans (St. Pancras main line) and Denham (Ex-GW&GC Joint from Paddington and Marylebone).

A youthful spirit of adventure, by pedal power, in July 1959 took me further than I had ever travelled on two wheels previously. I decided with a companion to cycle to South Wales in two days, with a break in the journey at Cheltenham overnight. The expression "Saddle sore" took on a new meaning during this epic journey!

Having reached Cheltenham by lunchtime, a memorable afternoon was spent in railway observation at Landsdown Junction[6]. This overlooked Landsdown station on the Midland route to Birmingham New Street via Bromsgrove and the Western route to Birmingham Snow Hill via Stratford-upon-Avon. The main Western Region stations in Cheltenham were Malvern Road and the terminus at St. James, branching right from the Snow Hill line shortly after Malvern Road station.

In the Gloucester direction the Banbury and Cheltenham railway also left the main line at Landsdown Junction and further divided shortly after Andoversford for the M.S.W.J.R. route to Andover. There was a great variety of traffic at Landsdown Junction which could be viewed from an overbridge very conveniently situated as an observation point for the junction. Commonplace were a liberal supply of Western and Midland locomotives together with the Standard types introduced following nationalisation.

The gem of the afternoon was, however, "Dukedog" 9005 from Oswestry running light in the Gloucester direction. I think she must have been going to Swindon Works and this may well have been her last journey.

Before the closure of the M.S.W.J.R., Southern engines reached Cheltenham, making Landsdown Junction quite a cosmopolitan crossroads. If my memory serves me correctly I saw "U" Class 31618 on this route. On the following morning we continued the journey to South Wales heading for the Rhondda Valley via Chepstow and Newport. This proved much more strenuous than the first leg of the ride to Cheltenham, but we made it in daylight!

During the course of the next few days we eventually reached Swansea, having visited the sheds at Neath Court Sart (87A), Neath & Brecon (Sub shed of 87A), Duffryn Yard (87B), Danygraig (87C), and Swansea East Dock (87D).

It was the many highly enjoyable interludes of observation, typical of Landsdown Junction that inspired the title for this book: *ONCE UPON A TIME BY THE LINESIDE*.

The railway habit is difficult to break and I still spend many pleasant hours by the lineside, if only to watch modern traction. Steam is, however, still very much "a magnet", particularly when in operation on the main line. The preserved locomotives, restored to a very high cosmetic standard, make smoke and steam spectacles that produce a warm glow of nostalgia even on the coldest Winter morning, bringing the memories of everyday steam flooding back.

The true sense of being beside a Western Region lineside continued from the early days of train spotting at Iver in the 1950's until the end of the diesel hydraulic era in 1973. I therefore, make no apologies for including a number of photographs of the last stalwarts of Western Region corporate identity in this collection; the "Westerns" Class "52" diesel hydraulics.

I hope this historical record will serve to encourage others to retrieve their notebooks from the loft and print those long forgotten negatives into further nostalgic reflections of the bygone railway scene.

ACKNOWLEDGEMENTS

I would like to thank my daughter, Alison, for her contribution in typing the manuscript between studies for her GCSE examinations, Barry Toms for proof reading and advice on preparation and presentation of the written matter.

My thanks go to all the British Rail (Railways!) staff, in particular the guides of Swindon Works during the last days of steam, who patiently waited for photographs to be taken before ushering the stragglers back to the main group. The staff at Iver station in the 1950's and 60's for putting up with the train spotters of the time, in particular for providing a safe haven in the office during downpours.

Finally, last but not least, my family for putting up with my hours in the darkroom and in preparation of the manuscript, together with all my friends for company by the lineside in both the bleak days of Winter and the long hot days of Summer.

If I could turn back the clock I would change nothing in my experiences during the last days of steam: Double-headers, pick-up goods, shed permits, whistles, exhaust beats, semaphore signals, rail joints and above all the steam engine. I am thankful for them all: Memories are made of these.

(opposite) **"Modified Hall" 7905 FOWEY HALL has just come off shed at Banbury to take over the 2.10 p.m. from Paddington on the 9th. June, 1963. 7905 was called upon to relieve a crippled D1011 WESTERN THUNDERER which followed the "Hall" into the station having lost a substantial amount of time. Photographs of both 7905 being prepared for duty and D1011 passing this same point are shown in chapter 9.**

TECHNICAL NOTE.

The classification of the ex-Great Western locomotives described in the Tables does not differentiate between sub classes and the parent class of the locomotive. Thus in the interests of clarification the following are an aid to identification:
(i) The "4200" class has a sub class of "5205", which have larger cylinders and detail alterations compared to the parent class.
(ii) The "4500" class has a sub class of "4575", which have larger side tanks, increased weight and detail alterations.
(iii) The "2800" class has a sub class of "2884" which differ by the addition of side windows in the cab and detail alterations.
Other classes have variations, but these are generally of a minor nature not worthy of separate distinction for the purposes of this book.

An early morning express bound for Wolverhampton smartly accelerates from Paddington with "King" Class 6028 KING GEORGE VI in charge. The Wolverhampton and Birkenhead expresses were shared between Wolverhampton Stafford Road and Old Oak Common depots. The majority were hauled by "Kings", but "Castles" were used on some of the services. During the modernisation programme to diesel traction on the Western and Midland Regions the services were gradually taken over by "Western" diesel hydraulics and Brush diesel electric type 4's.

1: WESTERN REGION TOUR 1960 - ROVER TICKET STYLE

By 1960 the West of England main line was in transition from steam to diesel traction, six years before the end of Western Region steam. Weekly deliveries of new diesel locomotives were slowly causing the ranks of steam engines to diminish, as each locomotive depot stored its redundancies nose to tail. In their places, proud, shining examples of the new, but short lived, diesel hydraulic era.

It was July, 1960 and time to fully experience the Autumn days of Western steam. With a companion, two Western Region rover tickets were purchased, which allowed seven days unlimited travel on the Western Region. We had decided to include as many visits to locomotive depots as could reasonably be arranged within the time schedule, organised some months previously.

Paddington on the morning of July 25th 1960 was still predominantly a steam stronghold with "5700", "9400" and "1500" classes of Pannier tanks busily tugging in coaching stock from Old Oak carriage sidings for the steady stream of morning departures. The 9.10 a.m. to Birkenhead was destined to be the first taste of steam travel. The booked motive power, 6025 KING HENRY III, would take the train as far as Wolverhampton. Our initial destination was Wrexham, where a visit to the locomotive depot at Croes Newydd was planned, following which we would retrace our steps to Shrewsbury, via Oswestry, to find bed and breakfast for the night.

Following an engine change at Wolverhampton, 7922 SALFORD HALL arrived at Wrexham on time after a pleasant but uneventful journey. Croes Newydd shed was host to thirty locomotives at the time of our visit of which "Dukedog" 9014 held the most affection and Eastern Region Class "J39" 64748 the most interest. Departure from Wrexham was achieved with 4946 MOSELEY HALL in charge of a train for Shrewsbury, but we were to break our journey at Gobowen for the push and pull to Oswestry to visit the small locomotive works and the locomotive depot.

Upon arrival in Gobowen, "1400" tank 1458 and two coaches were waiting patiently for the connection. Oswestry was only a short distance down the branch and the journey time with the 0-4-2T was only a few minutes. Both shed and works were visible from the station platform and in consequence were not difficult to reach. Of the twenty-four engines on shed, 7822 FOXCOTE MANOR has since been saved for preservation, and has been in operation at Llangollen.

There was little activity in the works but "5700" Class 9629 and "Midland" Class "2" 41201 were under repair. In store, after closure of the Welshpool & Llanfair narrow gauge line by British Railways, were 822 and 823. Happily they still survive as No.1 THE EARL and No.2 THE COUNTESS, thanks to the Welshpool & Llanfair Preservation Company Ltd.

Pushed by 1458, we returned to Gobowen to complete the days journey into Shrewsbury with 4994 DOWNTON HALL at the head of a train for Paddington.

On foot from Shrewsbury station the motive power depot was quite difficult to locate, but the aroma of Midland coal directed the way. The depot was divided into two sections, one housed the ex-Great Western allocation and the other the Midland. The Western engines outnumbered the Midland by two to one on that day.

Bed and breakfast was impossible to find, there being no room at the Inn at every potential resting place. Without more ado we decided to try and sleep in the station waiting room on the cold and hard wooden seats. Within two minutes of establishing a suitable bench we were accosted by the law requesting our intentions. Kipping in

the waiting room of Shrewsbury station was a cardinal sin in 1960 and our destination was demanded as we were escorted onto the platform. With good fortune we were pointed in the direction of the 3.48 a.m. to Aberystwyth, which must have been expecting us since the coaches were already in the bay at midnight! We had not managed to find this train on the station timetable; I imagine it was unadvertised as far as Welshpool. Who in their right mind would want to leave Shrewsbury at 3.48 in the morning? Trying to sleep, one on each side of the compartment with the night traffic plodding through the station was impossible, and we were glad when the coaches jolted as Mogul 5331 coupled up.

The train was practically empty and remained so for the best part of the journey across central Wales. Our train joined with another from Oswestry at Welshpool and 7822 FOXCOTE MANOR, which had been observed on Oswestry shed the previous day, chugged onward to reach Aberystwyth shortly after 7 a.m.

Following the Shrewsbury experience we decided to seek bed and breakfast after a chilly stroll along the sea front and a cup of warming tea in a cafe. On the second attempt suitable accommodation was found, and with peace of mind the day was now free to visit Aberystwyth and Machynlleth sheds together with a trip on the narrow gauge Vale of Rheidol railway. The weather, I remember, was less than favourable with drizzle and low cloud prevailing for most of the day.

Aberystwyth was a sub shed of Machynlleth and played host to ten engines on that damp Tuesday morning. Four of the locomotives were "Manors", which were rostered to be used on both the main line to Shrewsbury and the branch south to Carmarthen. Of the remaining six engines "4300" class Moguls predominated, one of which, 6333, would shortly take us to Machynlleth. Aberystwyth shed is now used to house the Vale of Rheidol locomotives.

Mogul 6333 retraced our early morning steps on the Cambrian through the isolated Dovey Junction station into Machynlleth. Only nine engines were on shed, which included "Dukedog" 9017, now running preserved as 3217 EARL OF BERKLEY on the Bluebell line. Another "4300" Mogul, 6353, returned us to Aberystwyth where we paid our respects to the Vale of Rheidol before retiring to bed early following the previous sleepless night.

Next morning the weather showed no improvement on the previous day, but this would not interfere with our journey on the 11.55 a.m. south to Carmarthen. I remember freshening up in the typically Welsh ornate jug and bowl on the dressing table of the bedroom before enjoying an ample helping of eggs and bacon for breakfast. Our train departed with Mogul 6316 in charge, a disappointment since we were hoping for one of the "Manors" noted on shed the previous day. The line to Carmarthen was one of the most picturesque in the country passing through the best of the Cardiganshire countryside. This is the home of the protected Red Kite, which circles over the green slopes of the mountains displaying its characteristic forked tail in search of food.

Arrival at Carmarthen was 2.25 p.m. and we decided to make immediately for Whitland by way of the 2.28 p.m. departure headed by 5905 KNOWSLEY HALL, a locomotive that was allocated to Goodwick. Engines from Goodwick were extremely rare visitors to the London division, most of their rostas remaining in Wales. It was unfortunate that insufficient time existed to make visits to the Pembrokeshire depots of Goodwick and Neyland since we had

Croes Newydd (84J) locomotive shed, (New Cross in English) was situated at Wrexham. This was the first shed visit of the 1960 rail tour. Among the engines on shed were "5600" Class 5651, which was in the process of having ash cinder removed from the smokebox and "5700" Class Pannier tank 8791 apparently ready for a turn of duty. Note the various shovels propped up against the corrugated shed, and the amount of ash piled high on either side of 5651 requiring removal, if only for safety reasons. Locomotives from 84J were very uncommon on the main line between Paddington and Reading. However, I remember on one pea-souper of a foggy morning, during an observation session at Iver station, "2800" Class 2878 from 84J emerging from the gloom, then to disappear again adding a cloud of steam to the fogs intensity. This made my day despite the appalling weather (the like of which we thankfully no longer experience) and with the greatest of satisfaction, having observed my last unseen "2800" Class locomotive, I returned home in the hope of better weather in the afternoon.

Welshpool & Llanfair narrow gauge railway 823 THE COUNTESS was photographed in store in the ex-Cambrian Railway workshops at Oswestry on 25th July, 1960. The locomotive along with its twin 822 THE EARL were stored following closure of the line by British Railways on November 5th, 1956 after a commemorative last train pulled by THE EARL traversed the line two days earlier. Almost one year after this photograph was taken THE EARL regained the narrow gauge tracks on July 28th, 1961, following intensive efforts by the Welshpool and Llanfair preservation society to reopen the line. There was much rejoicing in Welshpool at this event, when the townspeople living adjacent to the line adorned their properties with flags and bunting. Both THE EARL and THE COUNTESS are delightful little tank engines and are undoubtedly my favourite narrow gauge locomotives of all the "Little Trains of Wales".

Heading south to Shrewsbury, "Hall" class 4946 MOSELEY HALL passes Ruabon under a threatening sky. When I think of the poor lighting conditions, the speed of the train and the fact that I was leaning out of the window with a folding camera (against my better judgement and a practice not to be recommended, I was lucky to achieve a result at all). Ruabon was the junction for Barmouth and Pwllheli, the route taken by the 1963 Ffestiniog Railway A.G.M. special. On that occasion "A3" 4472 FLYING SCOTSMAN was intentionally relieved of command at Ruabon being replaced by a pair of "Manors". The lead engine was 7827 LYDHAM MANOR and the second engine, I think, was 7813 FRESHFORD MANOR, but I stand to be corrected on the latter. On the return journey the train smashed through level crossing gates in the dead of night, causing some delay to allow inspection of the track and examination of the train. This jolted everyone into a state of bewilderment until the cause of the thump and scraping noises became clear.

The overall roof at Shrewsbury created a depressing atmosphere as well as making photography difficult. Standing in the bay, shortly before the overall roof was removed, 7823 HOOK NORTON MANOR is anxious to forge its way into Cambrian territory with an early evening train for Aberystwyth. To the rear of the "Manor", standing in another bay, is "Black 5" 45399. Both locomotives appear to have a good head of steam. Most station environments were, and still are notorious for rubbish between the tracks. Shrewsbury was no exception and in consequence I have been forced to tone down the piece of newspaper lying in front of 7823, as it distracted attention away from the principal subject matter.

Standard Class 5 No.73021 was photographed facing the concourse of Swansea High Street station on July 27th, 1960. The engine has an 87F (Llanelly) shed plate having been transferred from Shrewsbury. Note also the SC plate affixed beneath the shed plate. This signifies that the locomotive has a self-cleaning smoke box. The Western Region had, in April, 1960, thirty-one of this class allocated to its depots. However more than half of these were Shrewsbury engines and were consequently often used on Midland Region territory.

programmed to be in Penzance the following morning. With little time to spare before the return departure from Whitland to Carmarthen, a hasty visit to Whitland depot was made, fortunately situated adjacent to the station. A small collection of tank engines were on shed, which included 6108 recently transferred from the London division.

Hawksworth "County", 1020 COUNTY OF MONMOUTH, returned us to Carmarthen, where upon we made our way directly to the motive power depot and found that our engine from Aberystwyth had arrived for servicing. Unexpectedly five "Manors" were present; we had expected to see the highest concentration of the class at Aberystwyth.

The journey east along the Towey estuary took us through Ferryside, where the ruins of Llanstephan Castle proudly occupy a hill on the opposite bank. As a child I remember playing on Ferryside and Llanstephan beaches collecting the attractive and colourful shells deposited at the high tide mark. We left the train, a diesel multiple unit, at Llanelly to find the locomotive depot. At this stage, notes we had made from a shed directory were put to good use as the shed was

a good brisk walk from the station. The shed contained thirty-nine engines including five Midland "8F's", no doubt from the Central Wales line, and a variety of pannier tanks.

We had planned to spend the night on the 9.35 p.m. Swansea to Penzance, scheduled to arrive in Penzance at 8.10 a.m. the following morning. Thoughts of another sleepless night ahead were on our minds as another multiple unit conveyed us into Swansea High Street in time to snatch a meal before boarding the Penzance train.

The 9.35 was full to the brim, leaving standing room only when we boarded the train, but many were to leave the train before Bristol and we hoped for an empty compartment to take a nap later in the evening. Motive power was "Castle" 5061 EARL OF BIRKENHEAD, which remained in command until we reached Cardiff whereupon a change was made in favour of 1011 COUNTY OF CHESTER. The "County" remained in charge until we reached Bristol in the early hours of Thursday morning. Although a large number of people had left the train an empty compartment could not be found. The train remained in Bristol for a considerable time enabling the arrival of

10

It was in the early hours of the morning of 28th July, 1960 that I first experienced the crossing of the Tamar via the Royal Albert Bridge. This was on the 9.35 p.m. Swansea to Penzance with the pride of the line, a "Warship" diesel hydraulic in command. Photography, was of course impossible on the train at that time of night, so I have included this shot taken many years later following the erection of the road bridge alongside. The photograph was taken from the Saltash side of the bridge. A magnificent view can also be obtained from the Plymouth side from a car park situated just below the skyline above the "Passengers must not cross the line" sign at the end of the down platform. The bridge was opened in 1859, commemorated by the inscriptions boldly displayed over the entrance portals at each end of the main spans. Brunel was seriously ill upon the opening ceremony of the bridge and in consequence he was conveyed across on a special truck drawn by one of Gooch's locomotives. Having seen his masterpiece completed he died a few weeks later.

the night postal to Penzance to be observed with a "Warship" diesel hydraulic at its head. Eventually another "Warship", D806 CAMBRIAN, buffered up to our train and we were soon heading west into the night and territory I had not had the pleasure of previously experiencing.

Exeter, Newton Abbot and Plymouth were all passed in a state of drowsiness until the familiar rail sound on terra firma noticeably changed. We were crossing the Tamar over Brunel's Royal Albert Bridge at Saltash, an experience which awoke me completely.

Penzance was reached within minutes of schedule, but this was not surprising considering the ample recovery margin at the principal stations en route. Little activity was evident in the engine shed at 8.30 in the morning, and surprisingly few engines were to be seen, but inroads into the steam allocation had already been made with five diesel hydraulics among the ranks of engines present.

Visits were planned to Truro, St. Blazey and Plymouth locomotive sheds for the rest of the day, before we could establish a suitable bed and breakfast staging post.

From Penzance to Truro our motive power was one of the original batch of "Warships", D601 ARK ROYAL, a rather unattractive brute, and from Truro to Par (for St. Blazey) we were double-headed by D6318 and D6322, type 2 diesel hydraulics that had been resident on Penzance shed the same day.

My personal interest was aroused by the sight of a further batch

of "Manors", by no means regular visitors to my home London Division territory in 1960. Two were observed at Truro and three at St. Blazey.

We were double-headed by another pair of type 2 diesels into Plymouth and with the help of the shed directory, and public transport, made our way to Laira (83D). Fifty-four engines were on shed including Southern "Battle of Britain" 34079 141 SQUADRON and eight mixed traffic "Granges", a class once used extensively in the West Country on all manner of turns. Unfortunately none have been preserved.

"Warship" D807 CARADOC took us on the next stage of the journey to Newton Abbot where a change of train was necessary for the Kingswear branch. Our motive power was 7014 CAERHAYS CASTLE at the head of a train into Torbay. We alighted at Paignton, which we had earlier decided as the best prospect of finding bed and breakfast among the rows of boarding houses in the town. Fortunately a suitable stop over was easy to find, and at a charge of fifteen shillings and sixpence seemed very reasonable.

The following morning showed a marked improvement in the weather after only spasmodic appearances of the sun since the start of the tour. Exeter and Newport were on the schedule before heading up the Rhondda Valley, north of Cardiff, to stay with relations until Sunday.

D812 ROYAL NAVAL RESERVE 1858 - 1959 pulled us from Paignton to Exeter, where a visit to the shed produced five diminutive

The Porth to Maerdy branch of the ex-Taff Vale Railway followed the valley floor of the smaller of the two Rhondda Valleys, Rhondda Fach. In its heyday the line had a healthy coal traffic from the many pits situated at each twist and turn of the valley. This view, taken from the down platform of Tylorstown station shows a Cardiff valleys three car diesel unit arriving with a train destined for Porth in the summer of 1960. The railway scene through the bridge, obscured in this photograph, framed Tylorstown Cynllwynddu No. 9 pit and its sidings. The winding wheel can be seen over the leading coach of the diesel unit. The pit has long since closed and the whole complex flattened. On this day a pair of "5600" tanks were in the yard and my hope was that one of the pair would depart prior to the arrival of the branch passenger, but this was not to be. The Maerdy branch closed to passengers in 1964, but coal traffic continued to the now closed Maerdy Colliery for another twenty-five years. In 1992 the line was still in situ through Tylorstown but the rails shine no more, ending the once proud tradition of Rhondda coal mining with its banked steam train formations and white billowing steam plumes, front and rear, reaching for the sky. Note the mile post visible over the fence proclaiming Tylorstown station was 18¾ miles from Cardiff Bute Rd, and the wooden planking at the platforms edge covering point rodding from the signal

"1400" class tanks, engines which were used on the Devon branches.

We were to experience another run behind 7014, this time as far as Bristol where a change was necessary for the run through the Severn Tunnel to Newport, achieved in fine style by 6842 NUNHOLD GRANGE. The two locomotive depots in Newport, Ebbw Junction and Pill, were a considerable distance from the station, and consequently public transport was necessary to reach them. Both depots were freight sheds with the smaller Pill shed catering for dock traffic. I remember a tank engine had derailed at the entrance to the shed blocking all movement. A strong complement of heavy freight "4200" class tanks were present in both depots.

There remained the journey to Tylorstown in the Rhondda Valley before a guaranteed good reception and the best nights sleep of the tour. 6821 LEATON GRANGE pulled us from Newport to Cardiff where we boarded a Barry to Treherbet diesel multiple unit into the Rhondda to experience the sight and sound of "5600" class tanks heading and banking heavy coal trains.

No plans had been laid for Saturday, but the prospect of travelling on the Rhondda and Swansea Bay line between Treherbet and Swansea proved overwhelming. I am glad that the opportunity wasn't missed since all that now remains is the track bed severed by the blocked 1 mile 1,683 yard Rhondda Tunnel under Bwlch mountain.

Sunday was the final day of the rover ticket. The way home we had chosen via Pontypool and Hereford, rather indirect, but there was time in the schedule to visit Pontypool Road and Hereford sheds.

Our intention was to proceed directly to Cardiff, but the train we boarded at Porth proved to be a Sunday extra diverging from the Taff Vale line at Treforest on to the ex-Barry Railway through Wenvoe into Barry Island, missing Cardiff completely. Despite the Barry delay, Pontypool was reached in good time with the assistance of 6903 BELMONT HALL. The locomotive depot was well patronised on that Sunday morning with sixty engines resident. We reached Hereford in the mid afternoon having enjoyed the drivers view of the advancing permanent way in the front seat of a d.m.u. An interesting selection of engines were on shed including "Jubilee" 45631 TANGANYIKA.

The last stage from Hereford to Paddington via Worcester was achieved with three changes of motive power. The locomotives involved were 5998 TREVOR HALL, 4910 BLAISDON HALL and 6983 OTTERINGTON HALL. The bustle of Paddington welcomed us back to home territory. A long standing ambition to tour the Western Region had been achieved and we were quite prepared to start all over again.

Tables 1-18 detail the locomotive depots visited during the tour and records their inhabitants at the time of each visit.

OBSERVATION RECORDS OF DEPOT VISITS IN JULY 1960.

25th July
Table 1. CROES NEWYDD (84J)
1600 Cl. 1659.
2251 Cl. 2294, 3207, 3210.
2800 Cl. 2871.
4300 Cl. 5318, 6306, 6339, 6357, 6380, 7314.
5600 Cl. 5651, 6610, 6632, 6694, 6698.
5700 Cl. 3749, 3760, 4683, 8791, 9793.
7400 Cl. 7409, 7414, 7428, 7431, 7433, 7442.
7800 Cl. 7817 GARSINGTON MANOR.
9000 Cl. 9014.
J39 Cl. 64748.
Total : 30.

Table 2. OSWESTRY (89A)
1400 Cl. 1438.
1600 Cl. 1602, 1628, 1668.
2251 Cl. 2264, 3200, 3208, 3209.
4300 Cl. 6342.
5400 Cl. 5421, 5422.
5700 Cl. 3600, 3789.
7400 Cl. 7410, 7417.
7800 Cl. 7822 FOXCOTE MANOR.
Cl. 2 46513, 46514, 46519, 46520, 46521, 46522, 46524, 46526.
Total : 24.

Table 3. OSWESTRY WORKS
W. & L. 822, 823.
5700 Cl. 9629.
Cl. 2 41201.
Total : 4.

Table 4. SHREWSBURY (84G)
1000 Cl. 1013 COUNTY OF DORSET, 1026 COUNTY OF SALOP.
2251 Cl. 2276.
2800 Cl. 2866, 3820, 3860.
4073 Cl. 5001 LLANDOVERY CASTLE, 5055 EARL OF ELDON,
5070 SIR DANIEL GOOCH, 5099 COMPTON CASTLE,
7008 SWANSEA CASTLE, 7026 TENBY CASTLE.
4300 Cl. 5322, 5331, 6317, 7301, 7309, 7336.
4900 Cl. 4959 PURLEY HALL, 4966 SHAKENHURST HALL,
4994 DOWNTON HALL, 5903 KEELE HALL, 5981 FRENSHAM HALL.
5700 Cl. 4623.
6100 Cl. 6144, 6159.
6959 Cl. 6964 THORNBRIDGE HALL, 6998 BURTON AGNES HALL,
7915 MERE HALL.
9400 Cl. 8499, 9463, 9472, 9498.
Cl. 3 40205.
Cl. 4 42307.
Cl. 5 42815.
Cl. 5 44748, 44835, 45143, 45190, 45422.
Cl. 8F 48468, 48660, 48737, 48738, 48739.
Cl. 5 73034, 73091, 73097.
Cl. 2 78005.
Total : 50.

26th July
Table 5. ABERYSTWYTH (SUB SHED OF MACHYNLLETH, 89C)
2251 Cl. 2260.
4300 Cl. 6333, 6340, 6342, 6377.
5700 Cl. 3630.
7800 Cl. 7802 BRADLEY MANOR, 7803 BARCOTE MANOR,
7815 FRITWELL MANOR, 7819 HINTON MANOR.
Total : 10.

Table 6. MACHYNLLETH (89C)
2251 Cl. 2204, 2233, 2286.
7400 Cl. 7405.
9000 Cl. 9017.

Cl. 2 78000, 78007.
Cl. 3 82000, 82020.
Total : 9.

27th July
Table 7. WHITLAND (SUB SHED OF NEYLAND, 87H)
1600 Cl. 1669.
4100 Cl. 4122, 4167.
4500 Cl. 5520, 5546.
5700 Cl. 3657, 8739.
6100 Cl. 6108.
Total : 8.

Table 8. CARMARTHEN (87G)
1600 Cl. 1648.
2251 Cl. 2216, 2217.
4073 Cl. 5067 ST. FAGANS CASTLE.
4100 Cl. 4132.
4300 Cl. 6316.
4900 Cl. 5902 HOWICK HALL, 5913 RUSHTON HALL,
5937 STANFORD HALL.
5700 Cl. 9606, 9632, 9666.
6959 Cl. 6967 WILLESLEY HALL.
7200 Cl. 7224.
7400 Cl. 7402, 7407, 7419, 7425.
7800 Cl. 7803 BARCOTE MANOR, 7815 FRITWELL MANOR,
7825 LECHLADE MANOR, 7826 LONGWORTH MANOR,
7829 RAMSBURY MANOR.
8100 Cl. 8102, 8103.
Total : 25.

Table 9. LLANELLY (87F)
1600 Cl. 1606, 1607, 1614, 1633, 1638, 1654, 1665, 1666.
4200 Cl. 4279, 5203.
4300 Cl. 5332, 7314.
4900 Cl. 5949 TREMATON HALL.
5600 Cl. 5656, 6653.
5700 Cl. 3642, 3698, 3713, 3719, 3761, 7765, 8726, 9743, 9788.
7400 Cl. 7400.
9400 Cl. 8467, 8474, 8477, 9485.
Cl. 4 42387, 42390.
Cl. 8F 48474, 48525, 48724, 48761, 48768.
Cl. 5 73037.
Cl. WD 90207, 90529.
Total : 39.

28th July
Table 10. PENZANCE (83G)
4073 Cl. 4087 CARDIGAN CASTLE, 5053 EARL CAIRNS.
4500 Cl. 4563, 4571, 5541.
6800 Cl. 6800 ARLINGTON GRANGE, 6801 AYLBURTON GRANGE,
6808 BEENHAM GRANGE, 6825 LLANVAIR GRANGE,
6860 ABERPORTH GRANGE.
6959 Cl. 7925 WESTOL HALL.
Type 4 D815 DRUID.
Type 2 D6312, D6318, D6319, D6322.
Total : 16.

Table 11. TRURO (83F)
4100 Cl. 4108.
4500 Cl. 4574, 4587, 4593, 5537.
5700 Cl. 4622.
6800 Cl. 6870 BODICOTE GRANGE.
7800 Cl. 7812 ERLESTOKE MANOR, 7813 FRESHFORD MANOR.
Total : 9.

Table 12. ST. BLAZEY (83E)
1000 Cl. 1002 COUNTY OF BERKS.
1600 Cl. 1626.
4200 Cl. 4294, 5264.
4500 Cl. 5539, 5557.

The western end of Machynlleth shed 26th July, 1960. "2251" class 2204 stands in the centre road with 2286 and 9017 facing shyly the other way. 2286, on the left, equipped with a very narrow tender, caused me some confusion in identification thirty years after the photograph was taken. Note the small accoutrements of the steam shed lying on the compacted cinder and adjacent to the shed building. Prominent are shovels, a wooden wheelbarrow, two sack barrows and what appears to be a buffer upturned, perhaps to make a seat! Machynlleth shed opened in 1863 and, following absorption into the Great Western in 1922, became MCH in the shed code notation used by the GWR. Following nationalisation the depot became 89C. Boundary changes in September, 1963 resulted in the Midland Region taking over the ex-Cambrian system through Machynlleth and the depot was recoded 6F, part of the Chester district coding group. The steam depot finally closed in December 1966.

Engines not requiring servicing at Landore shed (87E) were turned on Swansea High Street turntable, situated on a connecting line to the LNWR route into Swansea Victoria behind the east side of the station. In this photograph, taken from the centre platform of Swansea High St., 5039 RHUDDLAN CASTLE returns from the turntable in readiness for a working to Cardiff in the Summer of 1960. On the opposite side of the valley was the Swansea Vale Rly taken over by the Midland in 1876. The route can just be discerned from the signal post situated over the centre arch of the factory roof to the rear of 5039. The terminus of the ex-MR line was at St.Thomas out of view to the right of the locomotive. The prospect of observing a Neyland or Goodwick locomotive at High St. station was enticement to linger a while on the platform. Locomotives from 87H or 87J were a real bonus since visitations from these sheds were extremely rare in the London division. On reflection I can only remember seeing 5905 KNOWSLEY HALL, of Neyland, in the station and on balance Carmarthen or Cardiff saw more engines from these sheds than High St.

ST.BLAZEY cont.
4900 Cl. 4906 BRADFIELD HALL.
5101 Cl. 5193.
5700 Cl. 3705, 4665, 5744, 8702, 8719.
6800 Cl. 6816 FRANKTON GRANGE.
6959 Cl. 7929 WYKE HALL.
7400 Cl. 7446.
7800 Cl. 7806 COCKINGTON MANOR, 7816 FRILSHAM MANOR,
7820 DINMORE MANOR.
Type 4 D824 HIGHFLYER.
Type 2 D6308, D6321.
Total : 22.

Table 13. LAIRA (83D)
1361 Cl. 1363.
2800 Cl. 2861, 3862.
4073 Cl. 4095 HARLECH CASTLE, 5053 EARL CAIRNS,
5069 ISAMBARD KINGDOM BRUNEL, 5098 CLIFFORD CASTLE.
4300 Cl. 7335.
4500 Cl. 4591, 5531, 5532, 5572.
4900 Cl. 4920 DUMBLETON HALL, 4944 MIDDLETON HALL,
4945 MILLIGAN HALL, 5904 KELHAM HALL, 6913 LEVENS HALL,
6921 BORWICK HALL, 6938 CORNDEAN HALL.
5700 Cl. 3675, 3686, 3790, 4679, 6771, 9716.
6100 Cl. 6166.
6400 Cl. 6413.
6800 Cl. 6805 BROUGHTON GRANGE, 6823 OAKLEY GRANGE,
6829 BURMINGTON GRANGE, 6837 FORTHAMPTON GRANGE,
6845 PAVILAND GRANGE, 6849 WALTON GRANGE,
6860 ABERPORTH GRANGE, 6863 DOLHYWEL GRANGE.
6959 Cl. 7921 EDSTONE HALL.
7800 Cl. 7816 FRILSHAM MANOR.
Cl. BB 34079 141 SQUADRON.
Cl. 9F 92217, 92222, 92223, 92224.
Type 4 D600 ACTIVE.
Type 4 D804 AVENGER, D808 CENTAUR, D812 ROYAL NAVAL
RESERVE 1859 - 1959, D819 GOLIATH, D833 PANTHER.
Type 2 D6306, D6315, D6317, D6328, D6330, D6331.
Total : 54.

29th July
Table 14. EXETER (83C)
1000 Cl. 1007 COUNTY OF BRECKNOCK, 1023 COUNTY OF OXFORD,
1028 COUNTY OF WARWICK.
1400 Cl. 1434, 1451, 1462, 1468, 1471.
2800 Cl. 2882.
4100 Cl. 4105, 4117, 4136, 4150, 4176.
4300 Cl. 7311, 7316, 7335.
4900 Cl. 4924 EYDON HALL, 4942 MAINDY HALL,
4944 MIDDLETON HALL, 5932 HAYDON HALL, 5946 MARWELL HALL.
5700 Cl. 7761.
6400 Cl. 6406.
6800 Cl. 6813 EASTBURY GRANGE, 6874 HAUGHTON GRANGE.
6959 Cl. 6965 THIRLESTAINE HALL.
9400 Cl. 9480, 9497.
Total : 29.

Table 15. EBBW JUNCTION (86A)
1000 Cl. 1017 COUNTY OF HEREFORD.
1500 Cl. 1506.
2251 Cl. 2209, 2223, 2227.
2800 Cl. 2818, 2832, 3805, 3807, 3826.
4200 Cl. 4227, 4229, 4230, 4246, 4248, 4265, 4283, 4289, 4290, 4292,
5201, 5203, 5205, 5227, 5228, 5233, 5251, 5255, 5259.
4300 Cl. 5326, 6325, 6348, 7327.
4500 Cl. 5562.
5101 Cl. 5155.
5600 Cl. 5634, 5657, 6656.
5700 Cl. 3634, 3638, 3662, 3714, 3772, 4671, 7781, 7787, 8778, 9662,
9664, 9674, 9796.
6100 Cl. 6125.

6400 Cl. 6401, 6425, 6426.
6800 Cl. 6850 CLEEVE GRANGE, 6871 BOURTON GRANGE.
6959 Cl. 6967 WILLESLEY HALL.
7200 Cl. 7212, 7217, 7221, 7222, 7231, 7232, 7233, 7240, 7245.
9400 Cl. 9468, 9482, 9494.
Cl. 5 73023.
Cl. 4 75002.
Cl. WD 90149, 90544.
Cl. 9F 92000, 92001, 92007, 92225, 92229, 92230, 92235, 92242, 92250.
Total : 83.

Table 16. NEWPORT PILL (86B)
4200 Cl. 4214, 4235, 4258, 4259, 4276, 4280, 5200, 5202, 5235, 5244,
5250, 5252.
5700 Cl. 4643, 4682, 5768, 6724, 6739, 6752, 6760, 6764, 6775, 7721.
9400 Cl. 8440.
Total : 23.

31st July
Table 17. PONTYPOOL ROAD (86G)
2800 Cl. 2859, 2867, 2871, 2896, 3804, 3849, 3854.
4100 Cl. 4135.
4200 Cl. 4242.
4300 Cl. 5318, 6393.
4900 Cl. 4916 CRUMLIN HALL, 4955 PLASPOWER HALL,
4958 PRIORY HALL, 5940 WHITBOURNE HALL,
6921 BORWICK HALL, 6946 HEATHERDEN HALL.
5101 Cl. 5103.
5600 Cl. 5645, 5659, 5679, 5685, 5693.
5700 Cl. 3610, 3627, 3628, 3640, 3683, 3685, 3703, 3708, 3717, 3767,
3779, 4600, 4639, 4642, 4668, 5756, 5759, 5775, 5789, 7712, 7724, 7740,
7796, 8709, 8716, 8751, 9650, 9730.
6800 Cl. 6812 CHESFORD GRANGE, 6840 HAZELEY GRANGE.
6959 Cl. 7918 RHOSE WOOD HALL.
7200 Cl. 7227, 7230, 7246.
9400 Cl. 8493, 8495.
Cl. WD 90192.
Total : 60.

Table 18. HEREFORD (85C)
1400 Cl. 1445.
1600 Cl. 1617, 1657, 1662, 1667.
2251 Cl. 2241, 2242, 2249, 2295, 3201.
2800 Cl. 3824, 3828.
4100 Cl. 4115.
4300 Cl. 7326.
4900 Cl. 4913 BAGLAN HALL, 5917 WESTMINSTER HALL.
5700 Cl. 3728, 4657, 4659, 4678, 7771, 8781, 8787, 9665, 9717.
6800 Cl. 6878 LONGFORD GRANGE.
7400 Cl. 7418, 7437.
Cl. 6P5F 45631 TANGANYIKA.
Cl. 8F 48739.
Cl. 2 78004.
Total : 31.

In the foregoing list it is interesting to examine the locomotive movements from
shed to shed. For example:
2871 Croes Newydd on 25th July to Pontypool Road on 31st July.
4944 Plymouth on 28th July to Exeter on 29th July.
6342 Oswestry on 25th July to Aberystwyth on 26th July.
6921 Plymouth on 28th July to Pontypool Road on 31st July.
6860 Penzance on 28th July to Plymouth on the same day.
6967 Carmarthen on 27th July to Newport on 29th July.
7314 Croes Newydd on 25th July to Llanelly on 27th July.
7335 Plymouth on 28th July to Exeter on 29th July.
7803 Aberystwyth on 26th July to Carmarthen on 27th July.
7815 Aberystwyth on 26th July to Carmarthen on 27th July.
7816 St. Blazey on 28th July to Plymouth on the same day.
48739 Shrewsbury on 25th July to Hereford on 31st July.

I am not proud of the quality of this photograph but it does record the scene over the motive power depot at Truro (83F) and the station complex on 28th July, 1960. The weather was very dismal and my photographic equipment and ability of the day were not up to the demanding conditions. I was surprised to find just nine engines on shed in mid morning. Dominant in the photograph is "Manor" Class 7812 ERLESTOKE MANOR. She is facing the turntable which is out of the picture immediately below the footpath vantage point used for this photograph.

Exeter Motive Power depot was situated adjacent to the station. On the 29th July "County" Class 1007 COUNTY OF BRECKNOCK was one of three "Counties" on shed. To the rear of 1007 stands 1400 Class 1451, used for branch traffic in the area. The projections above the cab and boiler of the "County" were typical obstacles to good photography in depot yards. It seemed that the locomotive of your chosen photograph was always strategically placed to ensure growths from the boiler. The "Counties" were the only ex Great Western standard gauge tender locomotives to carry straight nameplates. It is a great pity that none managed to secure a future in preservation.

2: NO LOITERING AT IVER STATION PLEASE

There is nothing notable about Iver station, situated 14 miles and 60 chains from Paddington, either for its architectural merit or its train service. It was, however, between 1953 and 1966, only a short cycle ride from my home in the village, and provided many hours of railway enjoyment for myself and friends.

Iver station could more appropriately be called Richings Park (for Iver) since the station is sited one mile from the village on the fringe of a housing complex built between the wars. Richings Park is within the parish boundary of Iver and provides perfect commuter housing. There are four platform faces serving up and down main and the up and down relief lines, of which the main line platforms rarely come into use except during Sunday occupation of the relief lines. On the north side of the platforms a goods loop connects Iver and West Drayton goods yard, although the former is out of use.

In the 1950's and 60's train spotters were an undesirable element at Iver, since the leading porter was very proud of his station. He considered a group of youngsters collecting train numbers detracted from the appearance of his well cared for environment. In consequence we frequently suffered self imposed exile, at a safe distance, on a service road on the other side of the tracks, which nevertheless provided a fine vantage point to view the constant procession of trains. Failure to move promptly resulted in threats to call the local bobby to enforce evacuation. We felt this was undesirable since we had no criminal inclinations! The thought of "Tin Wiskers" (an affectionate name for one of the local policemen) bearing down upon us was adequate incentive to move on.

Whenever I pass the old train spotting locations I look to see if there are any modern day spotters, but there never is. It seems the draw of steam was the underlying reason why youngsters of the day became hooked on railways as a hobby.

On reflection it was understandable why the leading porter at Iver did not want his boundary fence to hang in loops from the pressure of feet, or have the path blocked for passengers by a small band of railway enthusiasts.

However, on one occasion we did have extreme pleasure in joining, by invitation, a retired senior railway official seated on the embankment overlooking the station. We all observed the trains, for most of the day, comfortably seated on foldaway chairs on the wrong side of the fence! I recall his stockbook had recorded every GWR locomotive introduced since 1900 and their corresponding depot changes to date. This was a goldmine of information.

Traffic at Iver consisted of "6100" class tanks hauling locals, plying between Paddington and Slough or Windsor, laced with a few more interesting workings. In addition there were the semi fast trains to Reading that did not stop at Iver, a timetable pattern that still applies today. One of the more interesting workings that stopped at Iver was the 8.07 a.m. departure to Oxford via High Wycombe and Princes Risborough. The train regularly arrived with a 4-6-0 express or mixed traffic type, frequently from distant depots. This must have been a turn that returned stray engines nearer home, for anything from a "Castle" to a "Manor" could be turned out.

The "6100" tanks were replaced by class "117" diesel multiple units in 1960, which were appreciated if only for the magnificent drivers view from the front seats on trips to Paddington. This was a totally new experience.

At the time of transition from steam to diesel on the local services, the semaphore signalling gave way to multiple aspect colour lights. It was a sad day when the signal arms were bent through ninety degrees to prevent sighting and the colour lights switched on. The metallic clunk of the lower quadrants of the up main and relief were heard no more. So to the signal box overlooking the goods yard and loop was demolished in favour of control at the Slough box.

A modest goods yard served a prefabricated concrete factory and wagon load coal for the local coal merchants together with other miscellaneous merchandise. In addition refuge sidings allowed the occasional "2800" 2-8-0 to deposit its train and travel light engine up the goods loop towards West Drayton. I could never understand this manoeuvre, but no doubt it was one of the reasons why freight sometimes took an age to reach its destination. I remember the Station Master at Iver, with a list of numbers in his hand, walking down to the yard in search of lost wagons!

Every weekday the pick up goods called to shunt the yard on its trip working to West Drayton, before returning to Slough down the relief line in the middle of the day. This was invariably a Slough based Pannier from either the "5700" or "9400" Classes, but more frequently sightings of "6100" tanks were made when the suburban services were dieselised releasing these tanks for other duties.

My records show that in 1958 the yard was also shunted on some Sundays. It is difficult to believe that traffic warranted this activity, but on 27th February and on 1st May, 9406 was observed shunting.

Although Sundays were poor days for traffic-flow observations at Iver, the Western habit of returning locomotives from Southall to their home depots on Sunday afternoons, coupled in multiple, created much interest. Typical examples were:

27th February, 1958 -
Four engines coupled: 2813, 4965 ROOD ASHTON HALL, 6381, 75026.
Three engines coupled: 3824, 6820 KINGSTONE GRANGE, 6835 EASTHAM GRANGE.
6th March 1958 -
Four engines coupled: 2813, 2860, 2815, 90167.
Two engines coupled: 6365, 48420.
1st May, 1958 -
Four engines coupled: 2861, 3803, 3806, 75003.
Three engines coupled: 6833 CALCOT GRANGE, 6844 PENHYDD GRANGE, 48475.

Friday 27th May 1958 was an eventful afternoon of observation: The up *CORNISH RIVIERA* passed Iver at 5.05 p.m. with mogul 5330, of Pontypool Road, in charge. The up *BRISTOLIAN* didn't appear to operate or at least was running extremely late. The down *RED DRAGON* was unusually double-headed by "Castle" 5052 EARL OF RADNOR and "Britannia" 70026 POLAR STAR. Another, unidentified, express was double-headed by "Castles" 5025 CHIRK CASTLE and 5057 EARL WALDEGRAVE.

A favourite pastime was to record the traffic passing through Iver during the years of transition from steam to diesel. I am rather glad I did, since reflecting upon the locomotives seen and the variety of traffic, it now makes interesting reading. *Table 19* shows the flow of traffic on an August Saturday in 1960 between 2.30 p.m. and 4.30 p.m. *Table 20* shows the demise of steam traction passing through Iver station between 7.30 p.m. and 8.00 p.m. on random weekdays between 1961 and 1965.

"Hall" Class 6923 CROXTETH HALL was photographed approaching Iver on the down relief line on a Saturday morning in October 1962. This "Hall" was a Reading (81D) engine and was a very common occurrence through Iver, both on freight and semi-fast rush hour traffic for destinations in the Thames Valley. Note the length of the train, in excess of fifty wagons; also that colour light signals had, by this time, already replaced semaphores. The fifth railway line from right to left is the up goods loop connecting Iver and West Drayton yards.

On a sunny 3rd September 1964, "2800" Class 2822 rumbles through Iver with a loaded ballast train on the up relief line. The "2800" Class consisted of 167 engines of which those numbered between 2884 to 2899 and from 3800 to 3866 had detail alterations and side windows in the cabs compared to the example photographed in its original form. The far siding behind the engine, upon which rests the coal wagon, was the unloading point for road vehicle pick up. Iver did not posses a goods shed.

(above and below) **27th October 1962 was a fine day for Newbury races. There was never a better way to travel to Newbury Race Course station than with the "Kings" of the Western road racing into the heart of Berkshire. The two photographs show consecutive down specials numbered Z10 and Z11 hauled by 6000 KING GEORGE V and 6005 KING GEORGE II respectively. I imagine "Kings" were chosen for these workings due to the length of the trains which consisted of thirteen or fourteen vehicles. It was also appropriate to use these locomotives for the Sport of Kings! This view, just to the east of Iver station, can no longer be obtained since the M25 passes directly over this point. In addition many silver birches have seeded on the embankment, presumably from the parent tree still in its youth shown in both photographs.**

TABLE 19 **SUMMER SATURDAY AFTERNOON AT IVER (BUCKS) IN 1960.** Traffic Flow between 2.30 p.m. and 5.00 p.m.

Time	Loco. No.	Name	Depot	Direction	Train Description
2.34	4977	WATCOMBE HALL	81D	Down	Semi-fast suburban
2.39	D835	PEGASUS	83D	Down	Parcels
2.41	6326		86C	Down	Empty coaching stock
2.41#	4932	HATHERTON HALL	83B	Up	10.40 a.m. Minehead - Paddington
2.47#	5029	NUNNEY CASTLE	83D	Up	10.35 a.m. Torquay - Paddington
2.52	7035	OGMORE CASTLE	85B	Up	11.45 a.m. Cheltenham - Paddington
2.52	dmu			Down	Suburban
2.55	4945	MILLIGAN HALL	82D	Down	2.30 p.m. Paddington - Weymouth
2.58	5061	EARL OF BIRKENHEAD	86C	Up	9.20 a.m. Carmarthen - Paddington
3.04	4088	DARTMOUTH CASTLE	85A	Down	2.35 p.m. Paddington - Weston-Super-Mare
3.06	70029	SHOOTING STAR	86C	Up	8.00 a.m. Neyland - Paddington
3.09	dmu			Up	Suburban
3.11	7004	EASTNOR CASTLE	85A	Up	11.10 a.m. Hereford - Paddington
3.14	dmu			Up	Suburban
3.14	dmu			Down	Suburban
3.17	5916	TRINITY HALL	84B	Down	2.55 p.m. Paddington - Fishguard
3.19	4957	POSTLIP HALL	84B	Up	Unidentified express
3.21	92211		81A	Down	Freight
3.24	5924	DINTON HALL	82B	Down	Empty coaching stock
3.27	5055	EARL OF ELDON	83A	Up	11.30 a.m. Torquay - Paddington
3.31	D823	HERMES	83D	Up	8.15 a.m. Perranporth - Paddington
3.33	D813	DIADEM	83D	Down	3.15 p.m. Paddington - Kingswear
3.39	D819	GOLIATH	83D	Up	8.35 a.m. Falmouth - Paddington
3.40	dmu			Up	Suburban
3.42	dmu			Down	Suburban
3.50	D816	ECLIPSE	83D	Down	3.30 p.m. Paddington - Penzance
3.50x	D8xx			Up	*TORBAY EXPRESS*
3.52	dmu			Down	Suburban
3.54	D811	DARING	83D	Up	11.15 a.m. Plymouth - Paddington
3.58	5054	EARL OF DUCIE	82A	Down	Milk empties
4.02	dmu			Down	Parcels unit
4.03	dmu			Up	Suburban
4.04	5042	WINCHESTER CASTLE	81A	Up	1.50 p.m. Bristol - Paddington
4.09	6973	BRICKLEHAMPTON HALL	81A	Up	12.18 p.m. Newton Abbot - Paddington
4.12	dmu			Up	Suburban
4.13	5099	COMPTON CASTLE	86C	Down	3.45 p.m. Paddington - Fishguard
4.15	D815	DRUID	83D	Up	9.20 a.m. St. Ives - Paddington
4.17	70016	ARIEL	86C	Down	*CAPITALS UNITED*
4.19	6956	MOTTRAM HALL	84G	Up	Freight
4.20	6150		81B	Down	Suburban
4.21	4080	POWDERHAM CASTLE	83A	Down	Unidentified express
4.25	6903	BELMONT HALL	86G	Down	Empty coaching stock
4.29	92240		81A	Down	Milk empties
4.30	dmu			Up	Suburban
4.34	dmu			Down	Suburban
4.36	92216		86C	Up	Parcels
4.40	D807	CARADOC	83D	Down	4.15 p.m. Paddington - Plymouth
4.41	90691		86C	Up	Light engine
4.43	dmu			Down	Suburban
4.52	dmu			Up	Suburban
4.55	dmu			Down	Suburban
4.58	dmu			Up	Suburban
4.59#	D820	GRENVILLE	83D	Up	10.00 a.m. Newquay - Paddington

Table Legend: dmu - Diesel Multiple Unit; x - Unidentified number (Train paths crossed); # - Refer to note

Depot Coding: **81A** - Old Oak Common; **81B** - Slough; **81D** - Reading; **82A** - Bristol Bath Road; **82B** - Bristol St. Philip's Marsh; **82D** - Westbury; **83A** - Newton Abbot; **83B** - Taunton; **83D** - Laira (Plymouth); **84B** - Oxley (Wolverhampton); **84G** - Shrewsbury; **85A** - Worcester; **85B** - Gloucester; **86C** - Cardiff Canton; **86G** - Pontypool Road.

Note #: Timekeeping was generally within plus or minus 7 minutes, but with three notable West Country exceptions:
10.00 a.m. Newquay - Paddington running 29 minutes late.
10.35 a.m. Torquay - Paddington running 20 minutes late.
10.40 a.m. Minehead - Paddington running 20 minutes late.

(right) **A Paddington to Slough local pulled by "Tanner Oner" 6117 eases its train into Iver station during 1960.** The colloquial name of "Tanner Oner", so fondly remembered by the schoolboys of the 1950's and 60's, took their nickname from the old sixpenny piece referred to as a Tanner. The "Oner" of course represented the second digit of the number series commencing 6100 to 6169. The majority of the 6100 Class were allocated within the London division for the local services in the Thames valley, but from time to time the odd example ventured much further afield to the western extremities of Wales at both Neyland and Goodwick.

(below) Swindon built "9F" 92207 eases a freight through Iver on the up relief line on 3rd September 1964. Faintly observed in the distance is an eastbound diesel multiple unit on the main line presumably due to the occupation of the slow line. This particular "9F" has been preserved on the East Lancs Railway and named MORNING STAR, a name previously carried by Great Western "Star" Class 4004 and latterly by "Britannia" 70021.

Not many tender engines called at Iver station on stopping trains, but on the 7th June 1962, "Hall" 6926 HOLKHAM HALL waits for the green flag with the 4.18 p.m. Paddington to Banbury. The working timetable covering this date made no provision for this train to stop at Iver. The reason it did so is therefore a mystery, unless a cancellation of one of the stopping services had occurred. A different viewpoint would have eliminated the goods loop signals protruding from the top of the boiler. Had I taken the picture today I would have moved further away and allowed the chimney to obscure it or taken a lower viewpoint.

6100 Class tank 6125 makes a smart departure from Iver yard with the local 'pick up' goods on the up goods loop on 3rd September 1964. These locomotives were relegated to these menial tasks following displacement from suburban services out of Paddington. King Estate Agents, a familiar landmark for travellers passing Iver can be seen to the rear of the station footbridge. In the front window I remember a diorama of Richings Park with some very well modelled trees, the secret of which would have improved my railway modelling technique of the time immensely.

7030 CRANBROOK CASTLE takes the 2.55 p.m. Paddington to Fishguard past Iver goods yard on 1st September 1962. Judging from the plume of black smoke the engine was burning coal not typical of Welsh steam coal. The shed cleaners have done a good job in keeping the locomotive in fine cosmetic condition.

This was one of the first railway scenes I captured on film with a cheap 2¼" square format camera. Equipped with a top speed of ¹⁄₃₀₀TH of a second I managed to stop "Hall" Class 5974 WALLSWORTH HALL east of Iver with an unidentified express on the down main in April 1960. The faster speed of the up express blurred its image. It is interesting to speculate on the names carried on the blurred destination board of the carriage. My interpretation is Paddington, Tenby and Pembroke Dock, which could place the train as the up *PEMBROKE COAST EXPRESS*. If this is the case the down train is likely to be an express to Hereford. However, there may be other options and without a 1960 timetable to hand my opinion rests.

TABLE 20 **DECLINE OF STEAM OBSERVATIONS AT IVER 1961-1965**

The following observations taken at Iver between 7.30 and 8.30 p.m. show the dramatic reduction in steam operations on random weekday evenings between 1961 and 1965. All other services have been excluded for the purposes of clarity.

Date	Time	Locomotive	Allocation	Description
21/8/61	7.30	5062 EARL OF SHAFTESBURY	Neath (87A)	Up West Wales
	7.36	4086 BUILTH CASTLE	Reading (81D)	Down Bristol
	7.42	6961 STEDHAM HALL	Old Oak Common (81A)	Down freight
	7.48	6139	Didcot (81E)	Up freight
	7.49	6959 PEATLING HALL	Old Oak Common (81A)	Down Banbury
	7.58	6920 BARNINGHAM HALL	Old Oak Common (81A)	Down freight
	8.02	4991 COBHAM HALL	Taunton (83B)	Up Penzance
	8.04	1012 COUNTY OF DENBIGH	Swindon (82C)	Down milk
	8.07	5958 KNOLTON HALL	Old Oak Common (81A)	Up parcels
	8.26	7033 HARTLEBURY CASTLE	Old Oak Common (81A)	Up Swansea
	8.29	6927 LILFORD HALL	Oxford (81F)	Down light engine
	8.30	6117	Slough (81B)	Up empty stock
23/4/62	7.30	6963 THROWLEY HALL	Old Oak Common (81A)	Down Cheltenham
	7.37	7013 BRISTOL CASTLE	Worcester (85A)	Down Hereford
	7.43	6959 PEATLING HALL	Old Oak Common (81A)	Up Easter relief
	7.46	3807	Newport (86A)	Up empty stock
	7.49	7031 CROMWELL'S CASTLE	Worcester (85A)	Up Hereford
	8.10	7921 EDSTONE HALL	Old Oak Common (81A)	Up empty stock
	8.10	7018 DRYSLLWYN CASTLE	Old Oak Common (81A)	Up Easter relief
	8.25	6842 NUNHOLD GRANGE	Stourbridge (84F)	Up Easter relief
8/6/64	7.45	4903 ASTLEY HALL	Old Oak Common (81A)	Down light engine
	7.45	7340	Didcot (81E)	Down freight
	8.03	6125	Old Oak Common (81A)	Up parcels
8/7/65	8.29	6156	Oxford (81F)	Down freight

(opposite top) **On the 26th September 1964, Brush built diesel-electric D1734, the most modern traction of the time, effortlessly glides through Iver on the up main. The train identification panel shows 1A20. This I believe to be an express from Weston-Super-Mare, being a Saturday. However timetable buffs of the era may be wiser than my notebook of the time would indicate. This locomotive was the first of the 500 strong Brush-Sulzer class 47 to be withdrawn when it was damaged beyond repair, less than a year old, some four months after this scene was captured, when it was involved in an accident at Coton Hill, Shrewsbury.**

(left) **The introduction of colour light signals on the main line from Paddington in the early sixties resulted in this poignant scene of the up main semaphore at the end of the island platform. The signal arms were bent through 90 degrees, lamps extinguished and colour light signals introduced. I remember the signals being left in this condition for some time. A rope is attached to the signal so that it would fall safely away from the up and down main line when dismantled.**

(opposite) **Diesel-hydraulic "Warship" D843 SHARPSHOOTER heads the Sunday 11.15 a.m. Paddington to Taunton on the relief line through Iver on 24th March 1963 whilst the down main was occupied with engineering work. The locomotive appears to be in superb condition but closer inspection along the trim line on the body side shows a large area of paint that has flaked away. Note the overhead power line warning panels applied in ten positions on the locomotive. The loop line signal guards the loop exit from Iver yard to West Drayton.**

Old Oak Common Pannier 3646 pulls the stock for the 8.30 a.m. Paddington to Penzance into Paddington's platform 3 on 21st April 1963. The station seems surprisingly inactive. However, two or three months later and the station would be a hive of activity at this time in the morning, with many holidaymakers leaving for the West Country. The cathedral-like roof of Brunel's train shed gives a grand and spacious character to the place. The central span, under which the Penzance train will depart, is 102 feet wide, the two smaller spans either side having a width of 68 feet.

On the 22nd September 1962 the *CORNISH RIVERIA EXPRESS* ran in two parts. This scene on platform 1 at Paddington shows the second train, which departed five minutes after the principal express at 10.35 a.m. bound for Kingswear. The train locomotive is "Castle" 5060 EARL OF BERKELEY, allocated to Old Oak Common (81A). There appears to be one lamp missing from its bracket, since an express would normally carry 'A' code headlamps, one on each lamp bracket over each buffer. I rather like the way the sun is glinting off the paintwork but this gave me a great deal of trouble during enlargement. The very contrasty negative required soft printing techniques and substantial burning in and holding back.

3: PADDINGTON, OLD OAK AND SOUTHALL

Whenever I planned a railway trip, taking advantage of the excursion rates, it was always from Paddington that I preferred to commence the journey, rather than one of the pick-up points nearer to my home. There were two reasons why I chose to do this. In the first instance Paddington was the best opportunity to gain a window seat, as the excursion trains were often well patronised and secondly, there was nothing to compare with starting the journey under Brunel's magnificent train shed that is Paddington station.

There never seemed a dull moment at Paddington with regular interval express services leaving at practically regimented times throughout the day. The South Wales expresses left at five minutes to the hour, the Birmingham and Birkenhead services ten past the hour, the West Country trains at half past the hour and those to Bristol, quarter to the hour. In addition there were the Worcester line and Cheltenham trains generally leaving at fifteen minutes past each hour.

I could never understand why the timetable planners of the time didn't use on the hour departure times for one of the principle destinations. At one time, when I was considering the railway offices as a potential career it was timetable planning that attracted me. No doubt had I followed this career path the reason would have become known to me.

The final decade of Western steam traction was also the era of corporate image, with rakes of chocolate and cream coaches and trains of individual identity. Thus most of the more important workings bore names relative to their destinations. The headboard identification proudly carried on the top of the smokebox door of the train locomotive.

In the Summer of 1963 the weekday departure list from Paddington was impressive with sixteen named expresses. The corporate image of the Western Region oozing from the railway scene of the day. I list below the named trains departing from Paddington each weekday.

Train	To
THE INTER CITY	8.20 a.m. Chester
THE ROYAL DUCHY	8.30 a.m. Penzance
THE BRISTOLIAN	8.45 a.m. Bristol
CAPITALS UNITED EXPRESS	8.55 a.m. Cardiff
THE BIRMINGHAM PULLMAN	10.10 a.m. Birmingham
CORNISH RIVIERA EXPRESS	10.30 a.m. Penzance
THE PEMBROKE COAST EXPRESS	10.55 a.m. Pembroke Dock
CAMBRIAN COAST EXPRESS	11.10 a.m. Pwllheli & Aberystwyth
TORBAY EXPRESS	12.30 p.m. Kingswear
THE BRISTOL PULLMAN	12.45 p.m. Bristol
THE MAYFLOWER	4.30 p.m. Plymouth
THE BIRMINGHAM PULLMAN	4.50 p.m. Wolverhampton
THE SOUTH WALES PULLMAN	4.55 p.m. Swansea
CHELTENHAM SPA EXPRESS	5.00 p.m. Cheltenham Spa
THE CATHEDRALS EXPRESS	5.15 p.m. Hereford
THE BRISTOL PULLMAN	5.45 p.m. Bristol
THE RED DRAGON	5.55 p.m. Carmarthen

The West of England trains listed also conveyed through carriages to other West Country destinations.

With the onset of complete dieselisation practically all of these names disappeared. I think perhaps because the coaches no longer carried destination boards and of location difficulties for the headboard, since modern diesels had no lamp brackets to hang the plates on.

This would seem to be one of the primary features on today's corporate image related railway scene that remains to be reintroduced, I hope this reflection is by way of encouragement.

Of the train locomotives on these prestige expresses, one remains firmly in my memory: Castle Class 5053 EARL CAIRNS. This was a regular engine for the *TORBAY EXPRESS*, for a period while allocated to Newton Abbot shed. She was kept in pristine condition and must have been a good performer to remain in charge of this train day after day. I often waited at Iver for this train to pass before going home for lunch after a mornings railway observation.

Many of the Paddington to Penzance expresses and those to Birmingham and Wolverhampton were the domain of the "Kings" until replaced by diesels. Not ten years after the last breath of steam wisped away into history in 1968, so too the diesel hydraulics in their turn were soon to be replaced by the predominating and rapidly expanding diesel electric fleet. The *RED DRAGON* was frequently a "Britannia" working with examples of the class allocated to Cardiff Canton shed. When the "Kings" were removed from the Wolverhampton and Penzance bound trains they enjoyed a short spell of life on the South Wales expresses resulting in reallocation of the "Britannia's" to other regional duties. Many of the Newbury Race specials were "King" hauled presumably to give the punters a taste of power and speed in anticipation of things to come at the race track.

Of the named locomotive types operating in and out of Paddington, the "Manors" were the most unusual. A "Manor" at Paddington was indeed a rare sight until the London division accepted transfers from other parts of the region in the final years of running down the steam fleet. Two "Manors", 7818 GRANVILLE MANOR and 7821 DITCHEAT MANOR were more regularly seen than any other members of the class. At a distance "Granges" could be confused for "Manors" since both locomotive types had raised footplating over their cylinders. Although common in the London division "Granges" were more often seen on freight and in consequence were not common motive power for the expresses.

An occasional Hawksworth "County" would visit Paddington. I rather liked these machines since they broke from the Great Western tradition of having curved nameplates and had straight ones instead. I remember COUNTY OF MONMOUTH and COUNTY OF WORCESTER being rare examples in the London division during my lineside years. The latter was the last member of the class left for me to see. She eluded me for many years until she arrived at Cardiff (General) with a parcels from West Wales during a days observation on the station.

'Foreigners' were also to be seen at Paddington, but usually for planned and specific reasons, such as "A3" 60103 FLYING SCOTSMAN on a Ffestiniog Society special in 1963 and Scottish based "Clan" 72006 CLAN MACKENZIE with another rail enthusiasts excursion.

The coaches for the express traffic were brought into the station from Old Oak Common carriage sidings mainly by panniers from the "1500", "5700" and "9400" classes. The exhausts of these little engines echoed loudly in the train shed as the heavy empty stock of Summer expresses were placed in each departure road.

Upon the demise of Western steam at the end of December 1965, it was left to the diesel hydraulics from the "Warship", "Western" and "Hymek" types followed by an increasing fleet of D1500 Brush locomotives (Class 47) to form the mainstay of express

"Warship" diesel-hydraulic D803 ALBION awaits departure from Paddington with the 8.45 a.m. to Bristol on the 21st April 1964. The locomotive is in desperate need of a repaint to improve its cosmetic appearance, with paintwork more susceptible to knocks than steam locomotives, patches would often flake away to bear metal. One feature of the "Warships" compared to modern diesels was the application of the locomotive number on the cab sides at each end of the locomotive. These locomotives, later known as Class "42" under the revised locomotive classification system, were built by both BR at Swindon Works and by the North British Locomotive Company. D803 was one of the Swindon built engines. None ever carried the 42 prefix to their numbers.

Station pilot duties at Paddington were, in the 1950's and early 1960's, the domain of "1500", "5700", "9400" and in the later years "4500" and "6100" classes. On 15th September 1962, attractively designed Hawkesworth Pannier 1503 stands at the end of platform 1 waiting for signals. The "1500" Class were originally designed for heavy shunting work, but a friend who was once a fireman, with experience on these locomotives, commented that they were better suited to the Paddington pilot duties due to restricted outlook from the windows and poor positioning of the brake and regulator. The lads on the platform seem more interested in me taking the photograph than in 1503. To the rear of the engine is the parcels platform practically end to end with platform 1.

"9400" Pannier 9477 on station pilot duties backs out of Paddington after departure of the 3.15 p.m. to Hereford on 15th September 1962. The engine would have brought the stock into the station from Old Oak carriage sidings and was no doubt returning for another such load, or perhaps she would have taken the empty stock from an arrival back to the carriage sidings for servicing; my records did not show her precise activity. Again the trainspotters at the end of the platform are showing little interest in the pannier; not so if this scene were to be repeated today.

On the 20th April 1963 the Ffestiniog Railway Society A.G.M. 'special' ran from Paddington to Portmadoc. To celebrate the Ffestiniog Railway centenary of steam traction 1863-1963. Preserved "A3" 4472 FLYING SCOTSMAN was chosen to pull the train between Paddington and Ruabon and the return to Paddington on the 21st. Here the A3 is backing out of Paddington on Sunday morning. I never tire of watching FLYING SCOTSMAN on special workings and since this first photograph of the engine, in 1963, I have waited many hours by the lineside, on the Settle & Carlisle and on the Stratford run from Marylebone, for second helpings. After alighting from the train in Paddington I walked the length of the special to examine the damage caused by the level crossing incident mentioned in an earlier caption. A series of long heavy dents on the sides of a number of coaches were evidence of the accident during the night.

motive power at Paddington. These were, of course, later to be joined by Class "50's" and HST's.

There was a small servicing depot complete with turntable at Ranalegh Bridge, situated on the left shortly after leaving the station, but the principal locomotive depot was at Old Oak Common (81A), which of course still exists, but without its quadruple covered roundhouse accommodation.

Old Oak was an awe inspiring place to visit with a large proportion of its allocation, which in 1959 totalled 173 steam locomotives, radiating around each of its four turntables. Round houses were magical places particularly when shafts of sunlight picked out locomotives simmering away the afternoon awaiting their next duty turn. There wasn't a more perfect place to record the occupancy of the depot than standing in the centre of the turntable. On the 24th July 1960, I recorded the steam engines incumbent on Old Oak Common which appear listed in *Table 21*. Three years later on 24th November 1963, I again recorded the engines on Old Oak, but this time included the numbers of the rapidly increasing diesel fleet, shown in *Table 22*.

After 1962 the demise of steam on the Western rapidly accelerated, resulting in a large number of spare and withdrawn locomotives, some with anti-deterioration covers tied over their chimneys. Old Oak was no exception and lines of locomotives accumulated in the sidings. This was particularly a sad sight made even more poignant by the removal of the names on the "Castles", "Kings" and "Halls" stored in the sidings at the front of the depot, presumably to prevent theft.

There was a worthwhile business for British Railways towards the end of steam in the sale of nameplates and of course the Great Western embellished most of their locomotives with cabside brass number plates. Those that were not brass were made of cast iron and were still much sought after, although less valuable.

I remember visiting a collector in the Harrow area soon after the mass withdrawal of Western steam locomotives, who had the foresight to rescue a large number of names and numbers of Western locomotives. There were so many numbers and so much weight hanging on the walls that his brickwork required to be strengthened with bulge protection measures. Among the numbers was Mogul 6301

which I had never seen, being the last of the "6300" series of the "4300" Class left unrecorded in my ABC of numbers.

Prior to the modernisation programme of 1958 ones favourite nameplate could be reserved, if available for sale, at a cost practically less than the delivery charge. I remember making application for a nameplate, but my letter must have gone astray for I failed to get a reply and to my intense regret I never followed it up. My friend on the other hand reserved three plates, and I suppose to his regret also, cancelled two of them when the price increased to £25 or so each. Oh! for the same opportunity today!

In order to identify the stored or withdrawn engines, the smoke box door number plates were often left in situ. These were somewhat less desirable at the time, particularly as prior to nationalisation the Great Western engines did not carry smoke box identification, but had their numbers painted on the buffer beam. Upon complete withdrawal, once the locomotives had reached Swindon for cutting up, some of the smoke box plates were also removed and one had to rely upon the stamped number on the motion, but this wasn't always totally reliable as some of the number impressions caused confusion, particularly if part of the motion was from a different locomotive.

Permits to visit Old Oak Common and other western depots were available from the Paddington offices of the Western Region. I remember eagerly awaiting the postman to deliver these treasured documents complete with disclaimer should you fall down one of the locomotive inspection pits, trip over a rail and fall into hot cinders or a similar mishap. Old Oak was the principal passenger locomotive depot for the London Division and Southall the principle freight shed. The latter still exists, part of which is now used to service and repair the locomotives for the main line steam operations out of Marylebone and Paddington.

The comings and goings of Southall shed could be viewed from a footbridge spanning the tracks halfway between the depot and the station. There were steps from the footbridge leading down into the shed yard, and a notice, warning of trespass, gave many a trainspotter second thoughts. It was only with a shed permit that I ventured down the steps past the cycle racks with their 'sit up and beg' cycles awaiting for each owners journey home, then straight on to the foreman's office to present the permit.

5963 WIMPOLE HALL, of Westbury shed (82D), stands at the buffers of arrival platform No.8 in Paddington with an express from Trowbridge in June 1963. Note the Pullman in platform 5. The clock under the platform 5 sign shows 10.06 a.m. At 10.10 the *BIRMINGHAM PULLMAN* departed, but steam traction must have deputised for the Blue Pullman diesel on this day.

I suppose the fact that one's name and address were known to the railway authority created an easygoing relationship with visitors to locomotive depots and freedom to wander around Western sheds, at one's own leisure, was usually freely granted, but with mandatory safety warnings. This was indeed the situation on my visits to Southall. I can only remember being conducted around Carmarthen shed and, of course, Swindon on works visits.

On the other hand Southern depot visits were more rigorously controlled, presumably due to the live rail dangers on the running lines where electric traction was used.

On a Sunday, there was always an anticipation of seeing something rare on shed when walking between the lines of locomotives in the six road covered accommodation. I suppose my most rewarding observation on 81C, in my view, was 7804 BAYDON MANOR hailing from Llanelly. As luck would have it there was a vacant space in front of the engine which enabled a photograph to be taken. The rear of the shed seemed to be a dumping ground for damaged locomotives and I remember seeing "Mogul" 6378 with a badly distorted front buffer beam and a pannier with its leading driving wheels removed.

Southall played host to regular visits of WD 2-8-0's and in the later days of steam Midland "8F's". The WD engines were either Western based or from Woodford Halse on the ex Great Central line. These large robust machines had a distinctive clank when in motion, the sound of which I cannot recall emanating from any engine of Great Western origin.

In November, 1958 there were forty-five Midland "8F's" allocated to Western depots of which thirty-two were allocated to either Shrewsbury or Swansea Victoria for use on the Central Wales line, the route to Crewe and on the North to West line. Of the remainder, nine were allocated to Bristol, St. Philip's Marsh (82B) and four were based on Pontypool Road (86G). The Bristol engines were frequently seen in the London division on freight workings and hence visited Southall. *Table 23* shows the locomotives present on a visit to Southall on 24th November 1963. Note the presence of three "8F's" strangely all from Midland sheds.

(opposite, top) **The 12.40 p.m. Penzance to Paddington faces the concourse at Paddington with D1034 WESTERN DRAGOON on 21st July 1975. It is interesting to compare this scene at Paddington with those taken in the 1960's. The lighting has improved and the style of platform numbering has been simplified.**

(opposite) **4080 POWDERHAM CASTLE at Old Oak Common on 30th September 1962. The shed yard looks very scruffy, in keeping with the poor external cleanliness of 4080. Most of the early "Castles" had radiused covers over the inside cylinders, but Powderham Castle had the later design of square covers when this photograph was taken. No doubt an authority on Castle class locomotives will be able to explain the reason why the later style was carried by this locomotive from the first series manufactured. Sister locomotive 4089 was similarly fitted.**

TABLE 21 **OLD OAK COMMON (81A) LOCOMOTIVE DEPOT - 24TH JULY, 1960.**

The following is a list of locomotives on shed at the time with 'visitors' shown by the adition of their home depot code in brackets. Those with their depot allocation uncertain, because they carried no shed plate on their smokebox doors, are denoted by a bracketed hyphen.

1000 Cl. 1010 COUNTY OF CAERNARVON (82C).

1500 Cl. 1503; 1504; 1505; 1507.

2251 Cl. 2210 (-).

2800 Cl. 2852 (82C); 2874 (86C); 2876 (86J); 3808 (86A); 3822 (86E); 3823 (81F); 3836 (86E); 3859 (86G).

4073 Cl. 4081 WARWICK CASTLE (82A); 4089 DONNINGTON CASTLE (-); 4096 HIGHCLERE CASTLE; 5008 RAGLAN CASTLE; 5014 GOODRICH CASTLE; 5032 USK CASTLE; 5037 MONMOUTH CASTLE; 5042 WINCHESTER CASTLE; 5054 EARL OF DUCIE; 5057 EARL WALDEGRAVE; 5060 EARL OF BERKELEY; 5066 SIR FELIX POLE; 5074 HAMPDEN; 5082 SWORDFISH; 5087 TINTERN ABBEY; 5090 NEATH ABBEY (82A); 5093 UPTON CASTLE; 5096 BRIDGWATER CASTLE (82A); 7011 BANBURY CASTLE (86C); 7017 G.J.CHURCHWARD; 7018 DRYSLLWYN CASTLE (82A); 7024 POWIS CASTLE; 7028 CADBURY CASTLE (87E); 7029 CLUN CASTLE (83A); 7032 DENBIGH CASTLE; 7036 TAUNTON CASTLE.

4300 Cl. 6314 (85D); 6348 (86A); 6373 (85B).

4900 Cl. 4922 ENVILLE HALL (82B); 5924 DINTON HALL (82B); 5952 COGAN HALL (85C); 5958 KNOLTON HALL; 5979 CRUCKTON HALL (81D); 5986 ARBURY HALL (82C); 6920 BARNINGHAM HALL; 6924 GRANTLEY HALL (81D); 6925 HACKNESS HALL (84B); 6942 ESHTON HALL; 6956 MOTTRAM HALL (81F).

5700 Cl. 3754; 4615; 4644; 8754; 8756; 8757; 8762; 8763; 8770; 8771; 8773; 9659; 9661; 9700; 9701; 9702; 9703; 9705; 9710; 9725; 9751; 9754; 9758; 9784.

6000 Cl. 6000 KING GEORGE V; 6002 KING WILLIAM IV; 6003 KING GEORGE IV (83D); 6006 KING GEORGE I (84A); 6009 KING CHARLES II; 6010 KING CHARLES I; 6012 KING EDWARD VI; 6015 KING RICHARD III; 6024 KING EDWARD I; 6028 KING GEORGE VI; 6029 KING EDWARD VIII.

6100 Cl. 6111 (81F); 6120 (-); 6121; 6132; 6141 (81C); 6145; 6157; 6158; 6168.

6800 Cl. 6830 BUCKENHILL GRANGE (82B); 6852 HEADBOURNE GRANGE (82B); 6879 OVERTON GRANGE (84E).

6959 Cl. 6962 SOUGHTON HALL; 6985 PARWICK HALL (85B); 6987 SHERVINGTON HALL (84A); 6990 WITHERSLACK HALL; 7903 FOREMARKE HALL; 7904 FOUNTAINS HALL; 7912 LITTLE LINFORD HALL, (84E); 7927 WILLINGTON HALL.

7800 Cl. 7808 COOKHAM MANOR (83A).

9400 Cl. 9410; 9411; 9416; 9418; 9419; 9423; 9479.

Cl. W 31916, (73C).

Cl. 8F 48475, (84C).

Cl. 7P 70023 VENUS, (86C).

Cl. 9F 92090 (16D); 92214 (84C); 92216 (86C); 92240; 92246; 92247.

Total : 126.

DEPOT CODING: **16D** Annesley; **73C** Hither Green; **81C** Southall; **81D** Reading; **81F** Oxford; **82A** Bristol (Bath Road); **82B** Bristol (St. Philip's Marsh); **82C** Swindon; **83A** Newton Abbot; **83D** Laira (Plymouth); **84A** Wolverhampton (Stafford Road); **84B** Oxley (Wolverhampton); **84C** Banbury; **84E** Tyseley; **85B** Gloucester; **85C** Hereford; **85D** Kidderminster; **86A** Newport (Ebbw Jct); **86C** Cardiff (Canton); **86E** Severn Tunnel Junction; **86G** Pontypool Road; **86J** Aberdare; **87E** Landore (Swansea).

TABLE 22 OLD OAK COMMON (81A) LOCOMOTIVE DEPOT - 24TH NOVEMBER 1963.

1500 Cl.   1500; 1504; 1506.
2800 Cl.   2842; 2852.
4073 Cl.   4098 KIDWELLY CASTLE; 5001 LLANDOVERY CASTLE; 5041 TIVERTON CASTLE; 5043 EARL OF MOUNT EDGECUMBE;
5056 EARL OF POWIS; 5060 EARL OF BERKELEY; 5065 NEWPORT CASTLE; 5070 SIR DANIEL GOOCH; 5076 GLADIATOR;
7006 LYDFORD CASTLE; 7009 ATHELNEY CASTLE; 7010 AVONDALE CASTLE; 7014 CAERHAYS CASTLE; 7015 CARN BREA CASTLE;
7017 G.J. CHURCHWARD; 7018 DRYSLLWYN CASTLE; 7020 GLOUCESTER CASTLE; 7021 HAVERFORDWEST CASTLE;
7025 SUDELEY CASTLE; 7029 CLUN CASTLE; 7032 DENBIGH CASTLE; 7034 INCE CASTLE; 7036 TAUNTON CASTLE; 7037 SWINDON.
4300 Cl.   6379.
4700 Cl.   4701; 4703; 4706.
4900 Cl.   4908 BROOME HALL; 4935 KETLEY HALL; 4962 RAGLEY HALL; 5919 WORSLEY HALL; 5957 HUTTON HALL;
5971 MEREVALE HALL.
5700 Cl.   3618; 3646; 3715; 3750; 4606; 4609; 4615; 8756; 8759; 8763; 9706; 9707.
6000 Cl.   6028 KING GEORGE VI.
6100 Cl.   6125; 6135; 6169.
6959 Cl.   6969 WRAYSBURY HALL; 6985 PARWICK HALL; 7918 RHOSE WOOD HALL.
9400 Cl.   8420; 8433; 8436; 9405; 9418; 9463; 9470; 9477; 9495.
Cl. 4   76041.
Cl. 9F   92002.
Type 4   D815 DRUID; D819 GOLIATH; D821 GREYHOUND; D822 HERCULES; D850 SWIFT; D852 TENACIOUS.
Type 4   D1002 WESTERN EXPLORER; D1008 WESTERN HARRIER; D1019 WESTERN CHALLENGER; D1020 WESTERN HERO;
D1041 WESTERN PRINCE; D1054 WESTERN GOVERNOR; D1061 WESTERN ENVOY; D1062 WESTERN COURIER;
D1064 WESTERN REGENT.
Type 4   D1682; D1683; D1684.
Shunter   D3031; D3032; D3598; D3601; D3956; D3962; D3965.
Type 2   D6326.
Type 3   D7005; D7023; D7058; D7059; D7060; D7065; D7076; D7078; D7089.
Total : 69 Steam + 35 Diesel = 104.

(right) **A sorry line up of withdrawn locomotives at Old Oak on 30th September 1962. From left to right "Castle" 5082 SWORDFISH; "King" 6029 KING EDWARD VIII; "Castle" 5084 READING ABBEY; "Hall" 5931 HATHERLEY HALL and finally another "Castle", 5036 LYONSHALL CASTLE. Note that the only identification remaining on the leading engine is its smokebox number plate, the brass name plates and side number plates having been removed to prevent theft. Some engines ran in revenue earning service in this condition in the final months of Western Region steam operation.**

(opposite) **Prairie tank 6128 was photographed adjacent to the Old Oak Common factory on a Sunday in 1962. This locomotive was withdrawn in April 1965, after satisfying the demands of commuters on the local services to Paddington for many years before being replaced by diesel traction. To the right of the locomotive is diesel shunter D3406. There appears to be a discussion in progress with regard to the course of action to be taken to effect a repair to the engine. The line upon which 6128 is standing leads directly into one of the four roundhouse turntables.**

I was very pleased to see a "Manor" inside Southall shed on 24th November 1963. No.7804 BAYDON MANOR, allocated to Llanelly, simmers alongside three diesel shunters, D3753, D3759 and D3961. I almost gave up printing this photograph; the intense glare from the roof lights and the rear entrance of the shed, coupled with the deep shadows inside, wasted ten sheets of 10" by 8" photographic paper until the correct degree of burning in and holding back was achieved.

TABLE 23. **SOUTHALL (81C) LOCOMOTIVE DEPOT - 24TH NOVEMBER, 1963.**

2800 Cl. 2841; 2851; 2856; 2893; 3854.
4300 Cl. 5380; 6378.
4500 Cl. 5508; 5545; 5569.
4700 Cl. 4707.
4900 Cl. 4944 MIDDLETON HALL; 4950 PATSHULL HALL; 4991 COBHAM HALL; 5917 WESTMINSTER HALL.
5700 Cl. 3620; 3633; 3665; 4608; 8752; 9642; 9726.
6100 Cl. 6110; 6132; 6165.
6800 Cl. 6823 OAKLEY GRANGE.
6959 Cl. 6961 STEDHAM HALL; 6967 WILLESLEY HALL; 6986 RYDAL HALL; 7910 HOWN HALL; 7922 SALFORD HALL; 7923 SPEKE HALL.
7800 Cl. 7804 BAYDON MANOR.
9400 Cl. 9406; 9415.
Cl. 8F 48010; 48027; 48088.
Cl. 9F 92207; 92240; 92245; 92250.
Shunter D3753; D3759; D3961.
Total : 42 Steam + Diesel = 45.

Southall shed clock on the 24th November 1963 times the photograph at 2.30 precisely. On display from left to right are "Hall" 4950 PATSHULL HALL; "6100" Class 6132; "Modified Hall" 6961 STEDHAM HALL; "2800" Class 2856 and "Modified Hall" 7923 SPEKE HALL. All the engines were in steam and no doubt were going to be the first away early on Monday morning.

"Modified Hall" 6987 SHERVINGTON HALL leaves Iver under Dog Kennel Bridge and heads for Langley on the down relief line. I have the train recorded in my notes as the 4.25 p.m. to Banbury. The photograph was taken in September, 1962. The engine is in dire need of a clean as the British Railways cypher on the tender is invisible. The bridge is locally known as Dog Kennel Bridge, the reason I believe to be attributable to an alsation that was usually on guard close by, where horticultural workers lived in mobile homes. A white alsation baring its teeth keeps anyone away! The junction bracket signal covered Iver goods loop together with the yard and the up relief line. Iver goods yard incorporated a refuge siding capable of holding 61 wagons.

There was a short lull in my photography of railways between 1969 and 1971 when the depression of losing the last steam locomotive encouraged me to consider other subjects for photography, but it proved impossible when I discovered there was life after steam! In this photograph, taken passing under Dover Road bridge leading to the Slough Trading Estate, "Western" diesel hydraulic D1038 WESTERN SOVEREIGN heads for South Wales. It was practice during the final years of the "Westerns", to display their numbers in the front indicator panel. During research into my notes I realised that the display was IC53 not 1053 which I was attempting to locate. The scene dates from 1st June 1971.

4: DOWN THE MAIN TO READING

Down the main to Reading was a favourite pastime during holidays and Summer Saturdays. The local service from my home station in Iver necessitated a change at Slough to a Reading bound outer suburban service that missed out a number of stations between Paddington and Slough including Iver. Alternatively, if an early start was made it was possible to connect with the 7.55 a.m. from Paddington to Swansea, which stopped at Slough departing at 8.21 a.m. arriving at Reading at 8.41 a.m. thirteen minutes faster than the all-stations local train.

The South Wales express would normally be a "Castle" turn and latterly a "Western" or "Hymek" diesel hydraulic during the transition from steam traction. I cannot remember individual engines, but no doubt they hailed from either Landore or Old Oak Common sheds.

At Slough the bay platform for Windsor was, and still remains, adjacent to the down main platform from which the South Wales express departed. The Windsor branch diverged southward immediately after the station passing the motive power depot (81B) in the process. Long since been demolished, the depot's allocation in 1959 consisted of 36 tank engines of which the "6100" class predominated. The "6100's" would happily travel either boiler or bunker first on their journeys to and from Paddington. I recall the "Shwee-wee-wee" sound the cylinders made as the locomotives coasted into stations to pick up commuters, then the spirited departure for their next port of call.

From the main line, Windsor could be reached from both eastbound and westbound directions, made possible with the provision of a triangle connecting the main line with the branch. This was put to good use in the Summer holiday season when Windsor became host to excursion traffic emanating from other regions in addition to home based regional excursions. It was not unusual to see B1's from Eastern Region metals turning on the triangle ready for the trip home. The western arm of the triangle, following removal of the track, has reverted to scrub and silver birch.

The large trading estate in Slough was a short distance down the main line from the station and once had its own industrial railway network operated by Slough Estates. I was fortunate to work in an office overlooking a number of sidings adjacent to the main road through the estate. Everyday, at 11 a.m., either Slough Estates No.3 or No.5, both Hudswell Clarke saddle tanks, would shunt the sidings. Each forward and reverse movement of the pistons would sound a bell on the running plate to warn traffic of its approach. These were delightful green liveried engines with a friendly driver and a hale and hearty fireman who carried the shunters pole over his shoulder as he guarded the road crossings. The crew were always ready to greet passers by with a friendly toot. It is my regret that these everyday occurrences were never recorded on film. Seeing No.5, now preserved on the Yorkshire Dales railway, in fine fettle brings back pangs of nostalgia and lost opportunities with my camera.

Burnham station is an oddity among the stations between Slough and Reading, having one island platform serving only the relief lines. It would have been quite appropriate to add "for Slough Estates" after the station name due to its proximity to the large number of factories.

A short distance further west, Taplow station still remains predominantly as it was in the heyday of steam with its lattice footbridge replete with G.W.R. insignia and dated 1883. Little has changed since the days of steam, except for the platform canopy removed from the up main and demolition of the down main building at the time of HST introduction. It was close to this site that the first length of GWR main line terminated on the Taplow bank of the river Thames near Maidenhead in 1838, prior to the erection of Brunel's Sounding Arch bridge to cross the river into Berkshire.

Maidenhead station was the junction for High Wycombe and the Marlow branch, now truncated at Bourne End, but still retaining the branch line skirting the Thames on its short journey into the attractive little town of Marlow.

The Marlow Branch auto train was affectionately called the "Marlow Donkey" and in 1973 the complete Maidenhead to Bourne End and Marlow branches were the scene of the 100th anniversary of the Marlow branch celebrations, with steam providing trips into history throughout the day. Three engines were used in the celebration, "6100" class 6106, "Modified Hall" 6998 BURTON AGNES HALL and "1400" tank 1466 which represented the "Marlow Donkey" for the day.

A journey between Maidenhead and Twyford always seemed never ending, but in reality is only five miles, a similar distance from Twyford reaches Reading (General) but the lineside interest seemed to make the journey shorter.

The Henley branch still leaves the main line at Twyford and in those latter days of steam travel had a healthy commuter service direct between Henley and Paddington, with fast runs after the Maidenhead and Slough stops.

Leaving Twyford the main line passes through Sonning Cutting with its high crossing bridges, passes the site of Erleigh Power station (now demolished), Sutton Seeds trial ground, now laid out in industrial factory blocks and finally the gasworks and the Huntley & Palmer biscuit factory site, the latter now Prudential offices, before entering Reading station.

Reading has a historical association with the three B's, Beer, Biscuits and Bulbs. Only the brewing industry now remains, albeit removed from the town site to a location adjacent to the M4 motorway at the Basingstoke road interchange. Sutton Seeds of which the trial ground, with its blaze of summer colour in acres of parallel lines greeted passengers to the outskirts of Reading, has now moved to the West Country, however still in Western Region territory. The once large Huntley & Palmer biscuit factory, which had fireless loco's shunting the yard, has been demolished turning the land over to retail superstores. Very little of the once large building complex now remains following the demolition of the main office block in 1991.

There were three stations and two locomotive depots at Reading prior to closure of the Southern Terminus in 1962. I will briefly mention the Southern system which terminated at Reading (South), adjacent to Reading (General), from which you could look down on the activity from the up main platform. The terminus had a regular service of electric units to Waterloo and a steam service on the Guildford and Redhill line, which diverged from the electrified lines at Wokingham, not far from Reading. The train spotters at the East end of General were able to observe the station pilot and the Guildford line steam motive power in the station, adding a little spice to the constant stream of Western Region main line traffic. Most of the engines hailed from Guildford or Redhill sheds, Reading virtually having no allocation to its depot located a little to the east of the station. The depot could be clearly seen from the carriage windows

This delightful rural scene at Ruscombe, near Twyford, in Berkshire has little changed today. This photograph was taken on the 16th of May 1964 and shows the West of England milk empties on the down main line with Warship D845 SPRIGHTLY in charge. There seems to have been a down line track replacement and ballasting programme, with the down main relaid with concrete sleepered flat bottom track.

of arrivals into Reading (General). I remember U's, N1's, W's and standard 4's predominantly, and the brief and often frantic observations to record the number of all visible occupants.

A connecting spur joined the Western to the Southern system which the Summer Saturday holiday traffic from the Midlands to Margate and Ramsgate used to reach Southern metals. These turns in the early sixties had a variety of motive power from Southern and Western stables, but the Western seldom turned out anything larger than a "Manor". The spur still exists but the Southern station and shed site became, following demolition, a car park before the new Reading station and concourse office complex was erected on the site and opened in 1989.

Reading (General) was and still remains the first principal junction station outside Paddington with a frequent service of fast expresses to Paddington, the South West, Wales and the Midlands. Trains as far north as Glasgow and Edinburgh are now in the timetable. The *WESSEX SCOT* is a current day example but is devoid of a locomotive headboard typical of the steam era.

The West of England route parts company with the main line to Bristol and South Wales immediately west of the station and after Reading (West) station, at Southcote junction, it separates from the Basingstoke connection to the Southern Region. At Southcote junction the Reading Central goods branch, which has since been lifted. also diverged and was latterly the domain of diesel shunters and the rarity of a Diesel Multiple Unit special on at least one occasion. Reading (West) station with its rather spartan appearance was used as the Reading stop for the cross country trains between the North, Midlands and the Hampshire and Dorset coasts. The trains now plying between these destinations, scheduled to stop at Reading, do so at the main station, reversing in the process. West station is still used for local services to Basingstoke and Great Bedwyn.

The steam depot, coded 81D, was situated in the triangle joined by Westbury line junction, Reading West junction and Oxford Road Junction; the same site now occupied by the diesel maintenance depot. The steam depot had a nine road straight shed, a small lifting shop and the normal coaling and watering facilities to be expected of an important junction locomotive depot.

In the spring of 1960 as the steam fleet was in the process of being run down the allocation was 73 locomotives inclusive of three class "08" shunters, at that time, of course, not classified in the five digit numbering system, but classified in the D3000- D4000 series. There were 19 "Halls", 5 "Modified Halls" and 15 "6100" 2-6-2 tanks on allocation. The "6100's" saw extensive service on the rush hour semi-fasts to Paddington and other local services in the Thames Valley. Of the four "Castles" allocated to Reading at that time one would often be engaged on down line pilot and standby duties at the General station and was usually held on the centre road between platforms 8 and 9. This was a good photographic portrait position and in consequence a number of different locomotives were '35 millimetered' from platform 8. On occasions a "Hall" Class 4-6-0 would substitute. I imagine the "Castles" were chosen for this duty due to the prospective long distance run required of the engine should a failure take place. On the other hand the up line pilot was normally of a lower classification and was held in readiness in the bay platform adjacent to the London end of platform 5. In the early 1960's this would frequently be a "Mogul" or a "Hall", although as the region became more dieselised "Granges" and "Manors" reallocated to Reading, having been displaced from other parts of the region, were more usual.

In the 1950's locomotives such as 6825 LLANVAIR GRANGE or 7817 GARSINGTON MANOR would have been rare "cops" for trainspotters on Reading (General) station. Even more so running up

4939 LITTLETON HALL, clearly acting as' down line standby locomotive' at Reading as she is carrying express headcode lamps, waits in the centre road between platforms 8 and 9 on 8th September 1962. The standby was normally a Reading engine but on this occasion the engine was allocated to Didcot. Judging from the external condition of 4939 perhaps this is as far as it would reach!

(right) **Displaced from the Central Wales line, "Manor" 7817 GARSINGTON MANOR is the showpiece of Reading (General) on 2nd March 1963. She is being admired by a younger generation while standing in the bay platform on up line pilot duties. Note the 'No.8' on the water column, perhaps indicating that it is the eighth water column at Reading, and the inscription, cast vertically on the column, which appears to read "G.W.R. Wolverhampton Aug. 1897".**

My records do not identify this "Warship" photographed in November 1963. I believe 1A74 is the 1.40 p.m. Weston-Super-Mare to Paddington which has stopped on platform 5 at Reading (General). The time is around 4 o'clock and the platform lights indicate that the light is fading. This required a slow camera shutter speed evident by the movement in the railman approaching the locomotive. Beyond the front of the locomotive is a tantalising glimpse of the station forecourt showing buses of the time and a rather empty skyline: Another photographic opportunity regretted.

TABLE 24. **READING (81D) LOCOMOTIVE DEPOT - SUNDAY IN SEPTEMBER 1962**

2251 Cl.	2212
2800 Cl.	2842; 2888; 3858.
4073 Cl.	5018 ST.MAWES CASTLE; 5067 ST.FAGANS CASTLE; 5076 GLADIATOR; 7006 LYDFORD CASTLE.
4300 Cl.	6391.
4900 Cl.	4921 EATON HALL; 4975 UMBERSLADE HALL; 5973 ROLLESTON HALL; 5982 HARRINGTON HALL;
	6903 BELMONT HALL; 6907 DAVENHAM HALL; 6933 BIRTLES HALL; 6955 LYDCOTT HALL.
5700 Cl.	4609; 9763; 9789.
6100 Cl.	6103; 6112; 6119; 6131; 6134; 6138; 6161; 6165.
6800 Cl.	6825 LLANVAIR GRANGE.
6959 Cl.	6959 PEATLING HALL; 6960 RAVENINGHAM HALL; 7906 FRON HALL; 7914 LLEWENI HALL; 7919 RUNTER HALL.
7800 Cl.	7808 COOKHAM MANOR; 7816 FRILSHAM MANOR; 7817 GARSINGTON MANOR.
9400 Cl.	8436; 8496; 9450.
WD Cl.	90486.
Total : 41	

the line to Paddington if a failure caused such a locomotive to be substituted on a London bound express.

At the western end of the station the bays used for the Basingstoke trains still exist. I recall REMEMBERANCE a Southern 4-6-0 arriving with one of the Southern main line connection turns from Basingstoke. This was prior to my interest in photography and never recorded on film as a consequence. I regret not having the opportunity to photograph the Southern locomotive hauled freights that took "King Arthurs" and "S15's" into Didcot via the Reading West and Oxford Road Junction. On occasion a Southern based locomotive would visit "81D", its smoke deflectors creating an incrongous presence amidst the GWR designed engines that were its stable companions for the day.

Reading was one of the stations where the traditional Great Western practice of slipping coaches took place. This operation was conducted on the up line No.5 platform. The objective of slipping was obviously to save the time of a station stop, but the Reading slip required the train to snake slowly into the platform from the up through line, (now two way working), slip at the West end of the platform and subsequently return to the main line for the remainder of the run to London. The slip coach usually came to a stand, conveniently, directly opposite the ticket barrier. A steam locomotive would then remove the coach after the passengers had detrained. Slip operations

were being phased out at the onset of my railway interest and I can only remember observing the operation once at Reading.

Until recent years the G.W.R. signal and telegraph works were situated adjacent to the station but at a lower level. In its heyday the facilities encompassed a sawmill, foundry, blacksmith's and carpentry shops which produced signals, signal boxes, locking frames and level crossing gates. In addition to the prime manufacture of signal and telegraph and associated equipment a thriving repair shop dealt with ATC equipment and the servicing and repair of company clocks and watches. In order to run an efficient railway the time must be the same from Paddington to Penzance or Birkenhead, a factor of great importance and often not receiving consideration by the general public. Alas the proud traditional skills at Caversham Road, Reading are no more, following the demolition of the buildings to make way for a G.P.O. building, warehouses and a multi-storey car park.

I now live only three miles from Reading and the station still has a magnetic attraction to me. The traffic remains varied and interesting with a healthy supply of locomotive hauled traffic despite the large number of HST, multiple units and Southern electrics using the station.

Table 24 shows the locomotives present at Reading motive power depot on a September Sunday in 1962.

(opposite) **Express freight 2-8-0 No.4704, carrying fitted-freight type 'C' headlamps, works hard on the approach to Reading (General) on 2nd March 1963. During peak Summer Saturdays when the locomotive department were hard pressed to find sufficient motive power, these very able engines were asked to cope with express passenger turns. The Southern lines into Reading (South) run parallel with the Western route and are situated adjacent to the Southern signal box to the right of the engine.**

(right) **"Modified Hall" 7900 ST. PETERS HALL, with steam to spare, takes the Reading station freight avoiding line with a train of vans on 2nd March 1963.**

(above) **Reading motive power depot was a feast of photographic opportunity as this full side elevation of "Modified Hall" 6966 WITCHINGHAM HALL indicates.** The photograph was taken on a sunny 9th June 1963. Reading GW shed consisted of nine straight roads, four of the roads making an exit at the rear of the building where the turntable was situated. I managed a number of visits to the shed between 1960 and 1964 but, strangely, never observed a locomotive being turned on the turntable. The depot was also equipped with a repair shop, which in this photograph is shown to the rear of the locomotive.

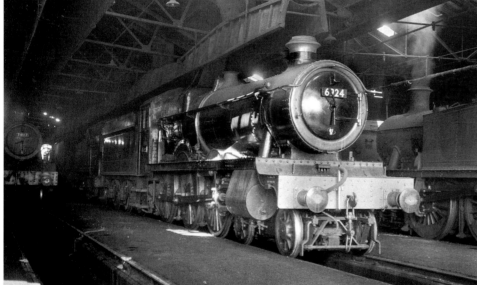

(left middle) **6924 GRANTLEY HALL** sparkles in "ex-works" condition inside the shed on 9th June 1963. To the left is 7817 GARSINGTON MANOR, and to the right a "6100" Class 2-6-2 tank. The photograph clearly shows the hazard that existed in locomotive sheds - inspection pits. I wonder how many broken bones were inflicted on employees slipping into the pits in this depot's history.

(left) **I particularly like this poignant picture of 6830 BUCKENHILL GRANGE** projecting its nose from a very dilapidated Reading engine shed on 2nd March 1963. The depot still had nearly two years to survive in steam operation and on this date its doors give the impression that an engine has forced its way through, breaking both sides simultaneously. I wonder if this was the case, or did they just fall into disrepair? The broken window panes and rusted casement speak a thousand words for the last days of steam engine sheds throughout the network.

I liked the juxtaposition of the locomotive and the water column when I took this photograph on 24th May 1964. 7808 COOKHAM MANOR stands outside the shed, on the road adjacent to the repair shop. A number of "Manors" were transferred to Reading following displacement from other parts of the region in the final years of the depot up to its closure in January 1965.

(right) The coal stage at Reading depot was situated at the rear of the shed. In this view taken on 2nd March 1963, Gloucester allocated "Hall" 6941 FILLONGLEY HALL stands alongside the stage. The pile of ash in the foreground of the picture is smokebox cinder and would have been removed by shovel from successive locomotives being serviced. Eventually the firebox and smokebox ash would have probably been shovelled into the adjacent wagon.

"Merchant Navy's" in Western territory were regular occurrences in the final years of steam. They worked from Bournemouth and Poole to Oxford and return. At Oxford they were replaced by Western or Midland Region based locomotives. In this photograph taken 19th June 1965, 35008 ORIENT LINE passes Cholsey and Moulsford signal box, on the up main, heading south. The benefit of smoke deflectors can be clearly seen as smoke swirls in front of the chimney and is carried away over the boiler top by the up draught generated by the deflectors. Little details taken for granted when the photograph was taken become apparent when studying the scene many years later. Two fire buckets, which would serve little purpose if the box caught fire, would today make a fine detail for a colour slide close up. A notice on the signal box door prohibits 'unauthorised entry'. On the signal box, at each of the four corners of the hipped roof, are ridge tile retaining metal scrolls that I like to think of as sparrow perches.

A scene all to often witnessed was the rescue of a "D9500" series diesel hydraulic following failure. In this situation "Western" D1046 WESTERN MARQUIS has rescued D9524 from Cholsey and Moulsford yard and is presumably taking the engine to Reading for attention. The "D9500" Class, introduced in 1964 for local trip working, had a short working life for British Railways. Many were sold to industrial concerns following closure of local rural goods facilities. Ironically this was fortuitous since a number have since been purchased from industry for preservation.

5: FROM READING TO DIDCOT AND OXFORD

The Worcester and Hereford expresses were among the last steam hauled passenger services from Paddington and it was one of these trains that I usually boarded for Oxford at Reading. Worcester shed were proud of their "Castles" among which, in the final Western steam years, were 5037 MONMOUTH CASTLE, 7005 SIR EDWARD ELGAR and 7007 GREAT WESTERN. Invariably one of Worcesters clean "Castles" would be in charge of the two-hourly interval service from Paddington to Worcester and Hereford commencing at 9.15 a.m.

On the exit from Reading the locomotive shed lay to the left and at a lower level, enabling the occupants to be viewed easily, but the large number of engines on shed caused any attempt at record taking to be impracticable.

Between Tilehurst and Didcot the Chiltern Hills present an attractive undulating landscape particularly colourful in Autumn.

Near the narrowest part of the Thames Valley, Goring troughs were the first opportunity for steam locomotives to replenish their water while on the move since leaving Paddington. Passengers quickly learnt not to lean out of the window over troughs, since an overfull tender sprayed water down the first three coaches of the train.

The Wallingford branch diverged at Cholsey and Moulsford, the track of which is still *in situ*. By 1965 the branch had closed for passengers, but remained open for freight to the Maltsters factory at the Wallingford end of the branch, until taken over by the Cholsey and Wallingford Railway Preservation Society. The society

headquarters is at Wallingford where heavy freight tank 4247 is in the process of restoration for eventual use on the railway. The line achieved light railway status in 1989 thus allowing services to be operated almost the full length of the branch with hopes that the eventual target of operating into the British Rail station at Cholsey will materialise.

During 1965 I chose Cholsey station to view the Summer Saturday procession of holidaymaker expresses still retaining steam traction albeit without Western based motive power. *(See table 25)*.

Continuing towards Didcot, South Moreton sidings lay on the right shunted by Didcot based pannier tanks. The sidings have long since been lifted. A short distance further at the junction town of Didcot the Oxford line parts company with the main line to Bristol and South Wales. Didcot steam depot (81E) was the main attraction for railway enthusiasts at this railway centre. However many of the expresses took the station avoiding line, which nevertheless gave an excellent view of the depot, if only in passing.

The Didcot locomotive depot buildings remain today much as they did when it was opened in 1932. It consists of a standard Great Western four road straight depot with a coaling stage and water tank over, repair shop and 65' turntable. However, additional buildings have been erected since B.R. closure commensurate with the growth of the preservation centre. An ash shelter once existed close to the coaling stage which prevented the glowing coals being observed from the air during the Second World War. Didcot was a target for enemy

---

TABLE 25. **CHOLSEY AND MOULSFORD - 19th June 1965.** Record of observations 2.00 p.m. to 4.30 p.m.

Time	Loco.No.	Locomotive Name	Direction	Train Description
2.01	dmu	—	Up	Local diesel unit
2.06	D1749	—	Down	Paddington to Hereford
2.11	D7080	—	Up	Cross Country (North to South)
2.20	45116	—	Down	Cross Country (South to North)
2.25	73083	PENDRAGON	Up	PINES EXPRESS
2.29	dmu	—	Up	Local diesel unit
2.35	D1021	WESTERN CAVALIER	Down	Paddington to Weston-Super-Mare
2.43	D1736	—	Up	Bristol to Paddington
2.43	dmu	—	Down	Local diesel unit
2.52	D1018	WESTERN BUCCANEER	Down	Paddington to Swansea
3.01	dmu	—	Up	Local diesel unit
3.02	D1748	—	Up	Hereford to Paddington
3.17	D1063	WESTERN MONITOR	Up	Swansea to Paddington
3.26	dmu	—	Down	Local diesel unit
3.36	73087	LINETTE	Down	Cross Country (South to North)
3.40	35008	ORIENT LINE	Up	Cross Country (North to South)
3.43	D1046	WESTERN MARQUIS	Down	Light engine (To goods yard)
3.50	D7062	—	Up	Parcels
3.59	34085	501 SQUADRON	Up	Cross Country (North to South)
4.03	D7081	—	Down	Cross Country (South to North)
4.10	D1713	—	Down	Paddington to Hereford
4.10	D1046	WESTERN MARQUIS	Down	Light coupled engines from yard
	D9524	—		coupled with D1046
4.17	45046	—	Up	Cross Country (North to South)

Note: For the sake of clarity the directional notation of the cross country trains are described as up and down as if to and from Paddington respectively.   *Table Legend:* dmu - diesel multiple unit.

(above) **In this final photograph at Cholsey and Moulsford, BR Standard Class 5 No.73083 PENDRAGON, one of twenty locomotives to receive nameplates based upon withdrawn Southern "King Arthur" Class locomotives, makes a sulphurous smoke screen as she races through the station with the *PINES EXPRESS* to Bournemouth on 19th June 1965. Note the scrollwork on the rather delicate looking station lamp standards and the stone bordered flower beds, still to be seen on many Western stations, of which Taplow comes to mind as typical.**

(left) **Two tone green Class "47" diesel electric, 1745, since renumbered 47152, was photographed held at signals near South Moreton in July 1972. The driver has just telephoned the box and is returning to his cab to await the green light. It is too much of a coincidence for the train identification to be 7V45 and the locomotive to be numbered 1745.**

This was the scene outside Didcot motive power depot on 9th June 1963. "2800" Class 2852 heads "Grange" 6868 PENRHOS GRANGE and a nose to tail line of "Hall" 4-6-0's. Identification between the "Grange" and the "Halls" in the line up is easy: Follow the footplate along the sides of the engines and the "Grange" clearly demonstrates that its footplate is raised over the cylinders.

bombers due to the proximity of the ordnance depot for which spark arresting panniers were provided, typified by their inverted conical chimneys. In common with many Great Western depots, Didcot had a sub-depot, albeit without covered accommodation. This was seventeen miles away down the Didcot, Newbury & Southampton Railway at Newbury. The meagre facilities of a pit and water tower were situated on a siding adjacent to the Lambourn branch platform.

The year of 1957 saw 3717 CITY OF TRURO, returned to service from museum exhibition, and it was allocated to Didcot seeing service along the D.N. & S. line. In the same year my first visit to Didcot took place during a break in a rail journey to Swindon locomotive works. It was Sunday and the prospect of a large locomotive presence was promising since Didcot was a quiet place on the Lords day. I remember observing a rank of simmering engines in front of the straight road shed; among them were "Halls", "Granges" and "2800" freights. Inside the shed "6100" tanks and "2251" 0-6-0's were among the occupants with smoke gently lifting into the roof space and out into the open air via the vents.

To the rear of the straight shed was the lifting shop and here a "4600" series pannier was partially dismantled for repair. In the sidings outside the repair shop a sundry collection of "Moguls", "Halls" and panniers buffered up to each other.

On each subsequent visit to Swindon, whether by rail or road, a break at Didcot was made to view the occupants of the shed, having previously arranged shed permits with the Paddington permit office. *Tables 26 & 27* list the locomotives present at Didcot on two occasions, in the first instance, in September 1960 followed by a Sunday in October 1962. Note the total absence of diesels despite the growing ranks of non-steam traction in the WR bookstock.

As the withdrawal of Western steam gathered momentum in 1962 a number of redundant engines were stored in the shed sidings, some of which were mothballed with sacking over their chimneys. Many would soon make the short journey to Swindon for cutting up. The depot itself closed in June 1965.

Modern Didcot, of course, houses the Great Western Society Museum of living steam which has grown to represent one of the major preservation bodies of Great Western steam in the country.

The centre has grown from the humble beginnings of occupying Taplow goods yard, when 6106 was the pride of their possession, still in the days when the remnants of B.R. steam were on their last passenger duties. Despite the praiseworthy efforts of the preservation movements, nothing can compare with the real thing on Sundays in the early sixties when not all the engines were clean, showing the efforts of the week, before taking a well earned rest on shed.

Upon leaving Didcot, quiet countryside followed through Appleford, Culham and Radley, the one time junction for Abingdon. Shortly after Radley, Kennington junction, which then connected the direct line to Birmingham with that through Oxford, heralded the outskirts of the city.

Oxford initially attracted me as a railway centre due to the prospect of observing locomotive changes on the cross country trains plying between the Midlands and the North to the coast of Hants and Dorset. At the height of Summer, Oxford was a busy station, particularly between 11.00 a.m. and 2.00 p.m. when southbound and northbound trains crossed each others pathing in the timetable. The variety of motive power on these trains kept the interest alive for many pleasurable hours of observation on those now far away days. Typical of the activity on an August Saturday in 1962 was the appearance of Southern "Merchant Navy" and "Battle of Britain" classes changing to Midland "Jubilee" Class and Black Fives or Western "Castles" "Halls" or "Granges". I remember much attention being paid to "Jubilee" 45581 BIHAR AND ORISSA of 55C Farnley Junction as it backed onto a northbound train on 20th July 1963.

When the motive power department were hard pressed to find suitable locomotives for the heavily laden holiday trains, "Manors" or Moguls would substitute for their more powerful shed companions.

Upon closure of the Somerset & Dorset joint line between Bath and Broadstone the *PINES EXPRESS* was re-routed via Oxford. The motive power on this once prestigious train was very varied. Most vivid in my memory was unrebuilt "West Country" 34102 LAPFORD and "Castle" 5026 CRICCIETH CASTLE on up and down trains respectively during the Autumn of 1962.

In the 1950's it was possible to observe locomotives emanating from the big four pre-nationalisation companies simultaneously at

TABLE 26. **DIDCOT (81E) Locomotive Depot** - Sunday in September 1960.

1400 Cl. 1447.
1500 Cl. 1501; 1502.
2800 Cl. 2819; 3856.
4300 Cl. 6363; 6379; 7324.
4900 Cl. 4912 BERRINGTON HALL; 4965 ROOD ASHTON HALL; 4969 SHRUGBOROUGH HALL; 5918 WALTON HALL; 5943 ELMDON HALL; 5944 ICKENHAM HALL; 5987 BROCKET HALL; 6915 MURSLEY HALL; 6937 CONYNGHAM HALL.
5700 Cl. 3653; 3704; 3751; 4615; 4649; 5746; 8720; 9754.
6100 Cl. 6109; 6113; 6124; 6136; 6139; 6149; 6153; 6159; 6164.
6959 Cl. 6993 ARTHOG HALL; 6996 BLACKWELL HALL.
9400 Cl. 8435; 8458; 9412.
WD Cl. 90573.
Total : 40.

TABLE 27. **DIDCOT (81E) Motive Power Depot** - Sunday in October 1962.

1000 Cl. 1007 COUNTY OF BRECKNOCK.
1400 Cl. 1445.
2251 Cl. 2201; 2221.
2800 Cl. 2834; 2856; 2898; 3819; 3840.
4300 Cl. 6309; 6350; 6357; 6363; 6379; 7324; 7327.
4900 Cl. 4994 DOWNTON HALL; 5987 BROCKET HALL; 6937 CONYNGHAM HALL.
5700 Cl. 3763; 4606; 5746; 8720; 9791.
6100 Cl. 6109; 6126; 6130; 6139; 6145; 6159.
6800 Cl. 6824 ASHLEY GRANGE; 6849 WALTON GRANGE.
WD Cl. 90573.
9F Cl. 92231.
Total : 34.

It is interesting to note that only ten of the engines listed were present on both occasions.

This ranks as one of my favourite photographs "On shed". It is Didcot on 10th March 1963 and "Hall" Class 4942 MAINDY HALL basks in the sun at its home depot waiting for its turn of duty. The lamps on the buffer beam indicate a passenger turn is likely, although express standby duties would also carry this code, as demonstrated in an earlier photograph at Reading. Sister engine 6937 CONYNGHAM HALL stands on an adjacent road. This was an extremely common performer between Didcot and Paddington. MAINDY HALL has returned to Didcot under the protection of the Didcot Railway Centre, but there is talk of converting the locomotive to a "Saint".

Oxford. There was, of course, the regular flow of Western traffic between the London division, Worcester and the Midlands together with the cross country traffic, both passenger and freight between South and North, bringing Southern and Midland locomotives into Oxford. The mix was caused by train engine changes, which for some was Basingstoke and others Oxford. This arrangement brought the foreigners to Western metals. *Table 28* shows the record of observations taken at Oxford on a Saturday afternoon in October 1962.

(opposite) **Didcot was a collection point for a large number of stored and withdrawn locomotives during 1963. Many of them were placed "in mothballs", with sacking over their chimneys to prevent ingress of foreign matter. This view, towards Didcot North Junction, taken from the tender of "County" 1007 COUNTY OF BRECKNOCK, shows "Hall" 5929 HANHAM HALL, "5700" Class 5746, "Castle" 5025 CHIRK CASTLE and "4300" Class 6379 all stored. Rather oddly 6379 has had its tender replenished with coal prior to laying in storage. Note that the sidings in the distance, between North Junction and Didcot station, are well laden with wagons. The station avoiding line, to the right of the engines, has now been reduced to double track.**

Although less prolific, Eastern engines managed to reach Oxford on the through York to Swindon, which was frequently a "B1" turn and also via the L.N.W.R. route between Oxford and Bletchley which carried through traffic from Cambridge. The "Oxbridge" line had its own terminus at Rewley Road adjacent to the Western station. From the north end of the up platform a grandstand view of the terminus and its environs were possible, since it was situated on a lower level to the Western through route.

Rewley Road closed to passengers in 1951 but the services to Cambridge continued using the Western station until the 30th December 1967. On that evening the passenger service, by then using diesel multiple units, ceased, leaving the route to Bletchley open only for freight. It was earlier, before the passenger turns were taken over by dmu's, that I saw my first ex-LNER D16/3 4-4-0 arrive at Oxford with a train from Cambridge. The pattern of services have turned full circle and passenger trains once again use the line.

The former LNWR terminus also had its own locomotive shed sited a few hundred yards north of a small swing bridge which created a throat leading to the station and goods yard complex. The shed was clearly visible from the northern end of the Western station, but I

"Modified Hall" 7920 CONEY HALL is eased on the approach to Didcot East Junction, on the Didcot station avoiding line, with a train to Paddington from the Worcester route in June 1963. The bald sky would have appreciated at least a wisp of steam, for there is no indication of movement in the photograph, but it was nevertheless worthy of the taking.

never saw the shed occupied. The depot no longer exists, neither does the Rewley Road complex, which has been converted to a car park.

The Oxford area was the one time junction for six routes, four of which still remain. Four diverged to the North and two South of the station. The main line from Paddington splits two miles north of Oxford into the Birmingham and Worcester routes and at Yarnton, a short distance along the Worcester line, the now closed Fairford branch diverged. The fourth route was the already mentioned Cambridge line. South of Oxford the Thame and Princes Risborough line forked eastward from the main line. The Morris motor vehicle works (now Rover), situated at Cowley, generated a healthy freight traffic in the bygone steam era, complemented with "6100" class tanks on passenger traffic. The line was also used as a relief route when the main line between Princes Risborough and Banbury was under engineering occupation.

In 1959 there were three "7400" Class Panniers allocated to Oxford, no's 7404, 7411 and 7412, which saw extensive service on the Fairford branch. Although I did not travel the branch itself I did manage a trip to Yarnton with 7411 with the object of viewing the occupants of Oxford locomotive shed in passing. The practice of using a branch line passenger train to view the occupants of railway installations was also carried out at Swindon where the Swindon Town branch train was boarded to obtain a preview of the engines outside the works on visiting days.

Hinksey Yard south of the station was the principle marshalling yard in the area which, prior to the rationalisation of freight handling methods was a hive of activity. "5700" Class panniers remarshalled incoming freight and relieved the train locomotives for running light to Oxford depot for servicing. A large variety of engines worked freight in the area: Midland "8F's" BR Standard "9F's", "Halls" and "2800" Class merely suggest the flavour of motive power regularly observed.

For some time before 1960 I pondered the whereabouts of the ex-G.W. steam shed despite the comings and goings of steam engines to and from the station. At the end of the down platform stood a rather rickety wooden structure which I believed to be a goods depot. It seemed that a fire hazard such as this could not possibly house steam locomotives. However, a shed visit confirmed this to be the depot, which, I am sure, had steam continued in the Oxford area after 1965, would have been a candidate for early rebuilding.

The cosmopolitan variety of engines to be seen on Oxford depot was as equally rewarding as a spell on the platform of the station. On the 9th June 1963, "Britannia" 70054 DORNOCH FIRTH was on shed, followed by, in September 1963, 70053 MORAY FIRTH. These were the only two "Britannia's" I saw at Oxford. I recall my companion taking pride of place in the drivers cab requesting his photograph to be taken in a classic pose at the cab window, which returned memories of his firing days at Southall depot, albeit on more mundane locomotives. *Table 29* lists the locomotives present on Oxford depot on the first day of September in 1963.

Oxford was one of the last locations on the Western Region where ex-Great Western engines were still to be seen running to the bitter end of Western steam. In the closing months of 1965 once proud and clean "Halls" saw their last days with name plates and number plates removed. Their grimy appearances contrasting with the whiteness of escaping steam emitting from every conceivable point of potential leakage due to the lack of either planned or preventative maintenance.

The station at Oxford is still an interesting place to while away a few hours observing the traffic. During the week there is a heavy concentration of Merry-Go-Round coal trains for Didcot power station and a healthy number of locomotive hauled passenger turns. Despite the absence of steam, a spell of observation at Oxford remains an enjoyable railway experience.

TABLE 28. **OXFORD STATION - 13th October 1962**. Record of Observations between 12.00 noon and 3.00 p.m.

Time	Arr/Dep.	Loco. No.	Locomotive Name	Direction	Train Description
12.04	Arr.	dmu	—	Up	Banbury to Oxford
12.20	Arr.	6818	HARDWICK GRANGE	Up	Worcester to Oxford
12.33	Dep.	7023	PENRICE CASTLE	Up	Hereford to Paddington
12.39	Dep.	7013	BRISTOL CASTLE	Down	Paddington to Hereford
12.49	Dep.	5076	GLADIATOR	Up	Wolverhampton to Margate
12.51	Arr.	dmu	—	Up	Cambridge to Oxford
12.56	Dep.	34102	LAPFORD	Down	PINES EXPRESS (Engine Change)
		5089	WESTMINSTER ABBEY		
1.08	Dep.	dmu	—	Down	Oxford to Bicester
1.20	Dep.	4979	WOOTTON HALL	Down	Oxford to Banbury
1.20	Dep.	6156	—	Up	Oxford to Princes Risborough
1.25	Dep.	dmu	—	Down	Oxford to Moreton in Marsh
1.30	Dep.	dmu	—	Up	Oxford to Paddington
1.35	Dep.	5085	EVESHAM ABBEY	Down	Margate to Wolverhampton
2.04	Dep.	5026	CRICCIETH CASTLE	Up	PINES EXPRESS (Engine Change)
		34102	LAPFORD		
2.15	Dep.	34104	BERE ALSTON	Down	Bournemouth to York
		6906	CHICHELEY HALL		
2.25	Dep.	dmu	—	Up	Oxford to Reading
2.26	Arr.	dmu	—	Up	Bicester to Oxford
2.32	Dep.	7031	CROMWELL'S CASTLE	Down	Paddington to Hereford
2.39	Dep.	7002	DEVIZES CASTLE	Up	Hereford to Paddington
2.46	Arr.	dmu	—	Up	Bletchley to Oxford
2.47	Dep.	6144	—	Up	Oxford to Princes Risborough
2.55	Dep.	dmu	—	Down	Oxford to Cambridge

In addition the following locomotives were observed through Oxford on freight trains:
2800 Cl.   3809.
4900 Cl.   4935 KETLEY HALL; 5987 BROCKET HALL.
6959 Cl.   7906 FRON HALL.
Cl. 5   44815.
Cl. 9F   92107.

Table legend: dmu - diesel multiple unit.
Note: The directional notation is again described as Up and Down as if to and from Paddington.

A fine study of "Tanner Oner" 6150, in a well used but sound condition, photographed at Oxford on 13th October 1962. The signal box behind the engine is Oxford station North which was open continuously in common with the South Box. Visible to the rear of the bunker of 6150 is the ex-L.N.W.R. engine shed for the Rewley Road Line into Oxford. The shed closed in December 1950 and all engine servicing was switched to the ex-Great Western shed on the opposite side of the line.

MUST
HE LINE
MEANS
BWAY

The route is clear ahead for **6910 GOSSINGTON HALL** as she makes a spirited departure out of Oxford heading for Banbury on 20th July 1963. There is nothing more to say about this picture - it speaks for itself!

(opposite top) **Following the end of the Summer service of 1962 the Somerset and Dorset route, south of Bath Green Park, lost its express passenger turns. This included the premier train of the line the *PINES EXPRESS* which was rerouted via Oxford. The *PINES EXPRESS* operated between Manchester and Bournemouth and was photographed arriving at Oxford on 13th October 1962. On that day 5026 CRICCIETH CASTLE was in command of the southbound run. An engine change was normally made at Oxford and on this occasion "West Country" 34102 LAPFORD exchanged command, allowing 5026 to go on to Oxford shed for servicing. The rear of the shed buildings dominate the left background, whilst on the right, behind the signal box, can be seen the erstwhile L.N.W.R. engine shed in an advanced state of dereliction.**

TABLE 29. **OXFORD (81F) Motive Power Depot**.
Record of observations - 1st September 1963.

1400 Cl. 1444.
1600 Cl. 1627; 1630.
2800 Cl. 2866; 2876; 3847.
4073 Cl. 7006 LYDFORD CASTLE; 7030 CRANBROOK CASTLE.
4900 Cl. 4922 ENVILLE HALL; 4975 UMBERSLADE HALL;
5928 WALTON HALL; 5924 DINTON HALL; 5955 GARTH HALL;
5960 SAINT EDMUND HALL; 5966 ASHFORD HALL;
5977 BECKFORD HALL; 5985 MOSTYN HALL;
6910 GOSSINGTON HALL.
5700 Cl. 3653; 4649; 9653; 9654.
6100 Cl. 6111; 6144; 6150; 6156.
6800 Cl. 6863 DOLHYWEL GRANGE.
6959 Cl. 6960 RAVENINGHAM HALL; 6970 WHADDON HALL;
7900 SAINT PETER'S HALL.
7400 Cl. 7404.
Cl. 5MT 45379.
Cl. 8F 48163; 48438.
Cl. 7P6F 70053 MORAY FIRTH.
Cl. 4MT 75022; 75055.
Cl. 9F 92246.
Total : 39

(right) **On the 9th June 1963, "Britannia" 70054 DORNOCH FIRTH was stabled at Oxford shed. The Pacific was a most welcome visitor, although by this time the engine had been re-allocated from its former Scottish base to Crewe and was now not too far off the beaten track. This was a powerful viewpoint to take a photograph of a "Britannia" and clearly shows the accessibility of the motion.**

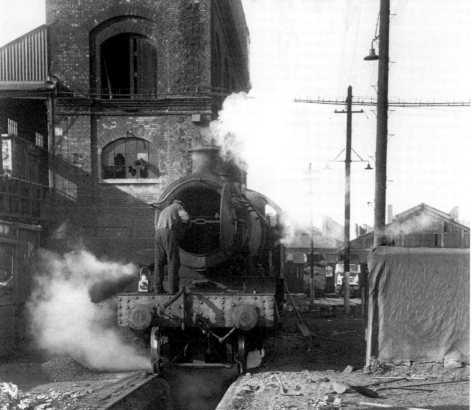

(above) **A study of a "4500" 2-6-2T at Swindon depot. When I took this photograph in 1961, 5536 had just arrived on shed and appeared to have steam to spare. On an adjacent track the first signs of transition from steam to diesel at Swindon manifests itself in the form of a new D63XX series diesel hydraulic.**

(left) **With the demise of the steam depot only weeks away in November 1964 an 'end of duty' servicing routine is being carried out on 5974 WALLSWORTH HALL with ash being removed from its smokebox. The two locomotives in the background are "2800" Class 3826 and "Hymek" diesel hydraulic D7001. On this occasion only three steam locomotives were standing outside the shed together with a variety of diesels. However the east roundhouse had twenty-one steam engines in residence which included four "Manor's" - 7808, 7813, 7816 and 7829.**

6: SWINDON FACTORY - LAST BREATH OF STEAM

In December 1840 the Great Western main line, under construction between Paddington and Bristol, was extended through Swindon and opened throughout to Bristol in June 1841. The first repair shops were commissioned at Swindon in January 1843 on a "green field site", a phrase which has now become familiar in modern industrial development.

Swindon was the junction for the Cheltenham Railway, which, together with its location as a suitable staging post represented the most appropriate site for the main GWR factory. Construction of locomotives was of course to Brunel's broad gauge standard, but when the gauge commissioners voted in favour of 'narrow gauge' (the current standard 4' 8½"), Brunel's system was doomed to eventual conversion.

In May 1892 final conversion to 'narrow gauge' was effected. The Concentration yard with its miles of sidings was built to concentrate broad gauge locomotives and rolling stock, which littered the yard with engines and coaches for conversion or scrap. In 1923 the Works was the birth place of Churchward's "Castles", the "Kings" in 1927 and the maids of all work, the "Halls" in 1928. After nationalisation, standard British Railways designed engines were constructed until the last steam engine built for BR emerged from the factory in 1960. The locomotive, "9F" 92220, was appropriately named EVENING STAR, but she was destined to have only a short existence in revenue earning service before her inevitable preservation.

The final years of steam precipitated an unprecedented level of railway enthusiasm. Railway clubs and societies organised excursions and visits to railway installations countrywide, and a new wave of 35mm photography captured the last breath of steam traction in photographic images of monochrome and colour.

Visits to Swindon Works were allowed for educational purposes and purely for enthusiasts by previously arranged permits. Sunday was the best day to choose for a visit because the helpful guides would tour the locomotive depot and the remoter parts of the works complex, where unexpected groups of engines were in repose, either stored out of service or awaiting the cutter's torch.

The queue outside the tunnel entrance in Bristol Street was often two or three hundred yards long waiting for the brisk euphoric bustle through the pedestrian underpass to the locomotive depot and the workshops on the opposite side of the tracks. All permits were handed in at the office, the numbers of visitors checked for illicit entry, security and safety, following which the tour commenced.

The view of the shed was sudden, having climbed the steps from the subway the party emerged near the throat of the depot. Expectations of a rewarding visit were frequently kindled by the sight of an Eastern or North Eastern Region "B1" simmering in front of the shed. This was in fact a regular visitor on the York to Swindon passenger and corresponding return working during the 1950's.

Standing on the turntable of the larger of the two roundhouses one could turn the body by slow degrees and catch the scattered shafts of sunlight illuminating a full compliment of engines ranging from "Castles" to saddle tanks. The more interesting designs warranted closer examination as did the rarely seen engines emanating from distant parts of the Western's system. A "Manor" from Machynlleth, or a "Grange" from Penzance, caught the attention and admiration of the onlookers.

The stragglers, and there always were some, were encouraged to follow the main party through the rear of the depot to the stock shed and associated sidings, which included those for the GWR gasworks. During the demise of steam, here rested redundant engines not always ready for the cutters torch, but with little prospect of a future. During a visit in 1961 the gasworks sidings held twenty-seven "9400" Class pannier tanks, which included 9400, now preserved and on display in the GWR museum in Swindon. Near the stock shed rested 4073 CAERPHILLY CASTLE prior to its main works overhaul for display in the Science Museum at South Kensington.

For a number of years there had been stories of a "Star" saved from cutting up. She was rumoured to be hidden somewhere in the Swindon Works complex and the stock shed was surely the most likely location. However the stock shed was frequently locked and access barred, but on one occasion a door had been left ajar and the temptation to see the hidden treasures proved irresistible. Inside a row of "Dukedogs" and a solitary "Dean Goods" rested with sacking over their chimneys, but at the end of one of the tracks stood 4003 LODE STAR with flaking paintwork casting aside her past magnificence. She was visibly complete in every respect and visions were conjured up of those magnificent machines in action during Great Western days. In later years the stock shed remained open for the inspection of its contents, but a small band of Class "03" shunters held no magical appreciation in the dying days of steam.

A return to the subway was necessary to gain access into the main Works area, thus avoiding crossing the Cheltenham tracks, albeit not particularly busy on a Sunday. The triangle, between the Cheltenham line and the main route to Bristol and South Wales, always held a variety of motive power awaiting admission to the Works or the concentration yard for cutting up. The main works offices overlooked the triangle where no doubt the fate of many an engine was decided.

From the triangle the main erecting shop was some distance along a service road, adjacent to the main line. The first hint of the type of engines in "A" shop was apparent by the tenders under repair in one of the buildings facing the main line. Approaching the works turntable the first "ex-works" locomotives came into view with copper capped chimneys and brass nameplates glinting in the sun. Soon these engines would make their way to the locomotive depot for running-in turns before dispatch to their home depots. There were a number of such trains, usually parcels or local passenger, on which expectations of seeing the unusual were always high. The sidings to the exterior of the Works held locomotives awaiting admission to the erecting shop for all classes of overhaul. Further "ex-works" engines were often on display to the passing trains and many others in sorry plight were making progress towards the ultimate indignation of the scrap heap. Some tank engines were reprieved for a brief period to act as Works shunters and many ex-Taff Vale tanks ended their career on these duties.

The interior of "A" shop (the main erecting and repair factory) was normally left until the concentration yard and the cutting-up shop ("C" shop) had been visited. This was no doubt to raise the spirits, having witnessed the pieces of metal left in heaps on the ground that were once the proud masters of the iron road. The concentration yard was usually the point of no return. Often over thirty engines, in nose-to-tail queues, occupied the yard waiting, in turn, to be moved to "C" shop for cutting up. On one occasion I observed 6000 KING GEORGE V in the yard, obviously an oversight since it was soon afterwards removed for preservation.

The main erecting shop was a magnetic place. The massive structure of the overhead traversing crane dominated the other machinery in the factory and overlooked the locomotives laid out in echelon over the full length of the shop. There could be six rows of locomotives in varying state of repair of erection, many with frames separated from boilers, others virtually complete following general overhaul, resplendent in a new coat of BR green or black paint. Simultaneous to the repair of steam locomotives, as the 1960's dawned, the erection of diesel hydraulics was in full swing. It was a sad scene to see the repair roads of "A" shop being taken over by these machines, but as time passes attitudes change and now the "Warships" and "Westerns" have joined the ranks of revered historical motive power.

There was much lingering in "A" shop and the guide had some difficulty in collecting the visitors into a semblance of an organised party before return to the outside world, away from the magnetism of the steam locomotive.

The carriage and wagon buildings at Swindon were earmarked for closure in 1962 and the work was subsequently transferred to the old locomotive works which were refurbished to accommodate the new activity. The locomotive depot closed in 1964 and was replaced by a diminutive structure near the station capable of housing a modest complement of diesel shunters.

In 1985 the 150th anniversary of the GWR was to be celebrated at Swindon with a grand exhibition of locomotives. As the date of the exhibition approached an announcement was made regarding the immediate running down of the Works and its eventual closure. The unbelievably bad timing of this announcement caused industrial action which prevented the celebrations from taking place, ending an era of railway history the like of which will never be seen again.

Table 30a and 30b record the locomotives present at Swindon Locomotive Depot and Works on 18th October 1964.

(opposite) **Shafts of sunlight pierce the deep shadows of Swindon roundhouse to highlight a trio of thoroughbred Great Western designed 4-6-0's on 10th April 1964. From left to right: "Castle" 7014 CAERHAYS CASTLE, "Manor" 7808 COOKHAM MANOR (since preserved) and "Grange" 6855 SAIGHTON GRANGE.**

(opposite, bottom) **Inside the roundhouse on 18th October 1964 rest "5700" Class Pannier 7782 and a smaller but younger variant "1600" Class Pannier, 1664. Also visible on the opposite side of the turntable is 7813 FRESHFORD MANOR. The end for the shed was very near and one wonders if the washout standpipes were ever again used.**

(below) **BR Standard 2-6-4T 80069 stands next to "Hall" 5943 ELMDON HALL outside the shed at Swindon on 19th August 1962. The Standard tanks were not scheduled for allocation on the Western Region following introduction in 1951, but towards the final years of steam, in the 1960's, a number of examples were transferred to Western sheds following displacement from other parts of the country. A batch, however, were allocated to Neasden from new and worked between Marylebone and Aylesbury via High Wycombe, on the ex GW&GC Joint, for a time.**

TABLE 30a: **SWINDON LOCOMOTIVE DEPOT - 18th October 1964.**

The following listing record the locomotives present at Swindon Works and locomotive depot on the 18th October 1964. This is not an official listing but a personal record of observations during a conducted visit and, is as complete as is reasonably practicable.

During the closing years of steam a great variety of locomotives were sent to Swindon for repair and cutting up. The following observations reveal former LNER, LMS and BR Standard design engines along with the expected complement of ex-Great Western motive power. In "A" shop, erection of the "D9500" series of hydraulics were half-way through the programme and heavy general overhauls of diesel hydraulics of the "Western", "Warship" and "Hymek" Cl.es were gradually squeezing the last breath of steam from the celebrated railway factory.

LOCOMOTIVE DEPOT (82C)
Steam
1000 Cl.   1012 COUNTY OF DENBIGH.
1600 Cl.   1658; 1664.
2800 Cl.   3826.
4073 Cl.   7014 CAERHAYS CASTLE.
4900 Cl.   4903 ASTLEY HALL; 5974 WALLSWORTH HALL.
5700 Cl.   3607; 4698; 7782; 9680; 9754; 9773.
6100 Cl.   6106; 6122.
6800 Cl.   6855 SAIGHTON GRANGE.
7800 Cl.   7808 COOKHAM MANOR; 7813 FRESHFORD MANOR; 7816 FRILSHAM MANOR; 7829 RAMSBURY MANOR.
4F Cl.   43940.
9F Cl.   92128; 92204; 92243.

Diesel
Type 4 (Cl. 52)   D1014 WESTERN LEVIATHAN.
Type 4 (Cl. 47)   D1712.
Shunter (Cl. 03)   D2126.
Shunter (Cl. 08)   D3512; D4119; D4120.
Type 3 (Cl. 37)   D6908; D6946.
Type 3 (Cl. 35)   D7001; D7018; D7067.
Shunter   15100.
Totals : steam 24; diesel 12.

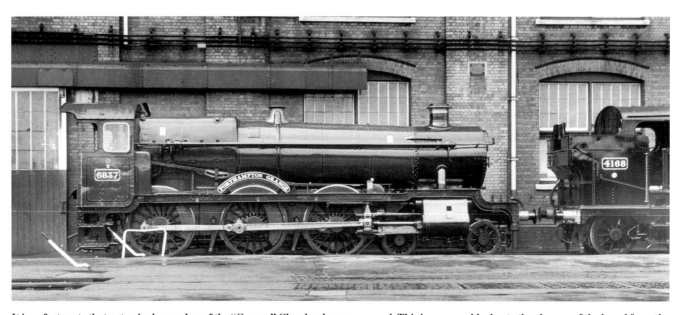

It is unfortunate that not a single member of the "Grange" Class has been preserved. This is presumably due to the absence of the breed from the scrapyards at Barry from whence the majority of todays preserved locomotives have emanated. For a short time following the end of steam there was a little wishful thinking among enthusiasts that a number had been collected together at a secret location to form part of a strategic reserve, hence their absence from Barry! The smaller driving wheels on these engines, compared to the "Halls", give rise to attractive side elevation proportions and necessitate the footplating to be raised over the outside cylinders. This can be clearly seen in this photograph of 6837 FORTHAMPTON GRANGE taken standing outside 'A' shop, following a major overhaul and a fresh coat of paint, on 10th March 1963. This was the first of the Penzance allocated "Granges" that I saw and in my experiences seemed to be the most likely of the Penzance "Granges", along with 6808 BEENHAM GRANGE, to stray from their home territory in the West Country.

TABLE 30b: **SWINDON WORKS - 18th October 1964.**

STOCK SHED

Shunter (Cl. 03)	D2088; D2146; D2186; D2187; D2192; D2193.
Shunter (Cl. 08)	D3824.
Cl. 14	D9515.

STOCK SIDINGS

4500 Cl.	4569; 4591.
5700 Cl.	3702.
4900 Cl.	4916 CRUMLIN HALL; 5963 WIMPOLE HALL.
6800 Cl.	6804 BROCKINGTON GRANGE.
Cl. 5	73012.

Totals : steam 7; diesel 8.

WORKS "A" SHOP

6800 Cl.	6823 OAKLEY GRANGE; 6827 LLANFRECHFA GRANGE.
6959 Cl.	7924 THORNEYCROFT HALL; 7929 WYKE HALL.
Cl. 5	42945; 42975.
Cl. 4	43001; 43012; 43120; 43137.
Cl. 5	73034.
Cl. 9F	92223.
Type 4	D604 COSSACK.
Type 4 (Cl. 42)	D806 CAMBRIAN; D815 DRUID; D817 FOXHOUND; D849 SUPERB.
Type 4 (Cl. 52)	D1006 WESTERN STALWART; D1010 WESTERN CAMPAIGNER; D1020 WESTERN HERO; D1060 WESTERN DOMINION; D1062 WESTERN COURIER; D1072 WESTERN GLORY.
Shunter (Cl. 08)	D3025; D3437; D3807; D3820; D3966.
Type 2	D6355; D6356.
Type 3 (Cl. 35)	D7017; D7027; D7064.
Cl. 14	D9516; D9517; D9518; D9519; D9520; D9521; D9522; D9523; D9524; D9525; D9526; D9527; D9528; D9529.
Shunter	15102.
Shunter (Cl. 97)	PWM 653.

Totals : Steam 12; Diesel 37.

WORKS - EXTERIOR SIDINGS

2251 Cl.	2210.
4200 Cl.	5257.
4900 Cl.	6951 IMPNEY HALL.
5700 Cl.	4659.
7800 Cl.	7803 BARCOTE MANOR.
9400 Cl.	8405; 8409; 9425; 9457.
Type 4 (Cl. 42)	D830 MAJESTIC; D843 SHARPSHOOTER; D860 VICTORIOUS.
Type 4 (Cl. 52)	D1032 WESTERN MARKSMAN; D1055 WESTERN ADVOCATE.
Type 2	D6330.
Type 3 (Cl. 35)	D7022.

Totals : Steam 9; Diesel 7.

"C" SHOP AND CONCENTRATION YARD

"C" Shop

Cl. V2	60856; 60916.

Concentration Yard

2800 Cl.	2818.
4200 Cl.	5264.
5600 Cl.	5602.
5700 Cl.	3748; 4626; 9752.
6000 Cl.	6000 KING GEORGE V; 6010 KING CHARLES I.
6800 Cl.	6873 CARADOC GRANGE.
9400 Cl.	8401; 8418; 9484.
Cl. 4	43003.
Cl. V2	60809 THE SNAPPER, THE EAST YORKSHIRE REGIMENT, THE DUKE OF YORK'S OWN; 60812; 60877; 60922; 60932; 60941; 60942; 60945.
Cl. 2	78009.
Cl. 01 (Ex-TVR)	28 (As National Coal Board No. 2 Area, Durham No. 67).

Total : Steam 25.

Grand Total : Steam 77; Diesel 64.

The date is 19th August 1962 and the place is unmistakably Swindon Works "A" shop. On that day "Castle" 7001 SIR JAMES MILNE receives attention to its front end. The pony truck and the buffer beam have been removed to expose the inside cylinders. To the right stands "9400" Pannier 9425, also receiving cylinder attention. During works visits I enjoyed searching out the numerous style of barrows and trolleys being used inside the various shops and yards. In this photograph are two heavy duty wheelbarrows, no doubt made somewhere in the Swindon complex many years previously. Above the engines runs an overhead traverser used for heavy duty lifting and movement of locomotive sections and components.

I doubt if the GWR could ever envisage the day that LNER "V2's" would be cut up at Swindon. On 18th October 1964 that is exactly what happened: 60916 was suffering the indignity of its transition to the scrap bins for conversion into something probably far less attractive than a mixed traffic 2-6-2 tender engine. On the same day, companion 60856 was also in the process of cutting up. In the concentration yard, outside 'C' shop, a further eight members of the class - 60809, 60822, 60887, 60922, 60932, 60941, 60942 and 60945 - languished awaiting a similar fate.

During the final years of steam overhaul at Swindon Factory, LMS Ivatt designed 2-6-0 engines were outshopped from the works. An example of this activity was evident on 24th May 1964 when 43044 was photographed, looking replendent, following a boiler and cab repaint. On that same day a further nine members of the same class were present. Simultaneous to the repair of these engines the "D9500" series of 0-6-0 diesel hydraulic locomotives were in the process of construction.

(above) **I believe the building in which 7005 SIR EDWARD ELGAR stands was called "The Barn". At least that is what it looked like, particularly as the side facing the works was open to the elements. This was ideally suited to let freshly painted engines dry off but I never saw any in there, only tired looking locomotives ready for overhaul or scrap. In front of the "Castle" is an ash pit, perhaps that explains the Barns true purpose?**

(right) **A fine sight outside "A" shop in 1963 was ex-works "5101" Class 4168 from Stourbridge Junction shed (84F). The "5101" Class were scheduled for limited main works repair during 1963.**

Condemned locomotives at Swindon were towed to the concentration yard before they met their turn of fate in the cutting-up shop. From left to right: "4300" Class 6348 and 7334, "5700" Class 8770, "6400" Class 6422, "2800" Class 2883 and "5700" Class 9727, 9744, 9759 and 9747 all wait their turn to fill the scrap bins on 10th March 1963.

Not many years were to pass before the diesel hydraulics that so proudly replaced the steam engine echoed the scenes of the 1960's at Swindon. On the 9th January 1977 this sad scene was repeated many times in the concentration yard, which was host to twenty four withdrawn examples of the "Western" Class. The number of the first locomotive is displayed in its route indicator panel. 1028 WESTERN HUSSAR heads the line-up of 1057 WESTERN CHIEFTAN, 1064 WESTERN REGENT, 1012 WESTERN FIREBRAND and 1025 WESTERN GUARDSMAN.

7: SOJOURN TO BRISTOL

One of the most prestigious expresses on the Western Region was the *BRISTOLIAN* which left Paddington at 8.45 a.m. and arrived in Bristol two hours later at 10.45 a.m. A similar schedule of two hours brought the return train into Paddington at 6.15 p.m. By 1966 the 8.45 a.m. from Paddington to Bristol, no longer known as the *BRISTOLIAN*, had been accelerated by ten minutes with a diesel hydraulic in charge.

The introduction of high speed trains had, by 1989, further accelerated the fastest run to 1 hour 21 minutes with stops at Reading and Bath included!

On the day that I decided to ride the Bristol line it was the 10.45 a.m. Paddington to Western-Super-Mare that I chose, in preference to the 'packed to the brim' *BRISTOLIAN*. Although steam was still very evident on the region it was a "Warship" diesel hydraulic, D850 SWIFT, that backed onto the train.

I had in mind to log the progress of the train with a stop-watch and to calculate its speed by mile post timings. I had discounted the rail joint method, which I remember was to count the number of rail joint sounds in 41 seconds. This result represented the approximate speed of the train in miles per hour. However problems existed at busy junctions or a sudden welded section when the change in sound confused the rhythm count. The prospect of high speed through Dauntsey or Box prompted my decision to time the train, but I was not expecting Bristolian type performance: just hoping!

Departure from Paddington was on time but acceleration slow, such that only 27 m.p.h. had been achieved by Westbourne Park. D850 continued a very sedate pace through Old Oak Common, passing the extensive carriage and locomotive sheds on the right. A number of 'Panniers' were marshalling stock in the yard and on the left, a Southern "W" type was shunting, a regular

visiting class to this yard. At Action yard more pannier tanks were marshalling incoming freight and a "2800" Class and a LMR "8F" were simmering after their journeys, their numbers obscured by lines of wagons.

Still only 55 m.p.h. through Ealing Broadway and I wondered if the "Warship" was in poor trim. We were down by 1 minute passing Southall depot where "4700" 4707 and "Modified Hall" 6973 BRICKLEHAMPTON HALL were among the line-up in front of the shed. Another speed check shortly after the station indicated a modest improvement to 57 m.p.h. An application of the brakes through West Drayton brought the speed down to 47 m.p.h. and three minutes behind schedule. Obviously the preceding train was slowing SWIFT'S progress. I remember thinking that I may be able to check the cause by reference to one of my fellow enthusiasts 'spotting' at Iver station, but no one was watching as the train ambled through the station on the down main. Pannier 9424, from Slough shed, was shunting Iver yard, shortly to leave Iver up the loop to West Drayton.

At last SWIFT began to accelerate, one minute had been recovered by Slough as we passed Horlicks at 65 m.p.h. still gently accelerating. Slough shed appeared dormant, probably because the suburban services to Paddington had been taken over by diesel multiple units. Slough (81B) closed in 1964.

Speed was steady through Maidenhead and Twyford at 71 m.p.h. The train was not scheduled to stop at Reading which was gained one and a half minutes down on schedule. The "Warship" headed into the heart of the Thames Valley picking up speed from 68 to 73 m.p.h., which she maintained until the outskirts of Didcot. The permanent way gang had been at work on the down main and a

Bristol Temple Meads in June 1963 had already become a mecca for the modern diesel hydraulics of the day and most of the passenger trains, by this time, had been taken over by diesel traction, particularly services to the West of England and to London. Steam was the exception not the rule. This "Warship" photographed at the western end of the station is a Plymouth Laira engine, confirmed by the 83D shedplate on the buffer beam. Unfortunately the locomotive must remain unidentified as steam photography was the principal purpose of my visit, but the lack of steam traction at the station encouraged me to record a number of diesel images on film without making notes on the subject matter. This was a cardinal photographic sin and I now realise that the mundane subject of the day becomes tomorrow's interesting history.

One of the few steam engines observed at the station on my June 1963 visit was 6873 CARADOC GRANGE, photographed running light through the station. The direction of steam flow and the way the crew are facing indicate that she is reversing. Later in the day I saw her at Bristol St. Philip's Marsh (82B) shed.

On that same June day in 1963, this view of Bristol Bath Road shows the encumbants of the locomotive depot at precisely two and a half minutes to one. Dominant in the scene are two "Warships" and a "Peak". Almost hidden from view, to the left of the group, a "Hymek" waits for a turn of duty. Not a steam engine in sight, since the shed was closed to steam on 12th September 1960 for rebuilding and was reopened on 18th June 1962 solely as a diesel depot.

The car registration plates date the scene to the 1970's but the appearance of Bristol Temple Meads had little changed from ten years earlier. Originally the station tower had a spire incorporated but this was destroyed during a German air raid on the city in 1941. The smaller corner spires are also remodelled compared to the original 1878 structure. Comparing this with early photographs I must confess that the German bombing improved the appearance of the tower, at least, for my taste. The tower and its pinnacles play host to starling roosts in the autumn. Black clouds of swirling birds sweep over the station like locusts and smother every possible perch space to roost for the night.

'permanent way restriction' slowed us down to 15 m.p.h. We were now running four minutes behind time. Speed had picked up to 57 m.p.h. through Steventon and further acceleration through Wantage Road and on to Challow at 70 m.p.h.

At Wantage Road the Wantage tramway once connected the ex-Great Western station to the town, 2½ miles distant. This was a standard gauge line operated by the diminutive 0-4-0 tank engine SHANNON, which was, at the time of my journey displayed on Wantage Road station platform. The line had closed at the end of 1945.

Challow station held a minor significance to me since it was a stopping off point for a break during the many road journeys made to Swindon Works armed with Sunday afternoon visit permits. I had not realised at the time that Challow was the site of the first serious railway accident on the GWR, way back in its infancy in October 1840, when Challow was known as Farringdon Road. The accident occurred when a night train headed by FIRE KING failed to stop at Farringdon Road station and crashed into the engine shed beyond the platform, killing the driver and injuring four others. At that time Farringdon Road was the temporary terminus of the London division of the GWR until the line was opened to Wootton Bassett Road a few miles west of Swindon in December, 1840.

With a speed that could only be described as moderate we continued through the Vale of the White Horse through Uffington, the junction for Farringdon, and on to Shrivenham. The Farringdon branch closed in 1963 and Uffington closed to passengers in 1964.

After Shrivenham speed increased to 77 m.p.h. and continued at this rate through Stratton Park where a small halt served a growing housing complex.

Swindon had a sudden impact as green fields gave way to sidings and factories after passing under a road bridge at Stratton Park. The Highworth branch, which closed in August 1962, diverged to the right and I remember a banana depot on the left.

The first stop for the 10.45 a.m. from Paddington was at Chippenham, so only a fleeting view of the works complex was possible and recording numbers of locomotives at 75 m.p.h. proved a little difficult, but I remember "Castle" 5006 TREGENNA CASTLE and ex-works "County" 1019 COUNTY OF MERIONETH outside 'A' shop and also observing a number of long lines of withdrawn locomotives in the concentration yard. Only the chimneys, cabs and domes being visible over a wide assortment of condemned rolling stock. The Swindon complex ended as suddenly as it began after Rushey Platt Junction, the connection with the ex-MSWJR line passing through Swindon Town.

We were now dead on time at Wootton Bassett as we diverged from the South Wales main line and headed for Dauntsey at 75 m.p.h. A down grade at 1 in 100 at Dauntsey held hopes for higher speeds. We attained 81 m.p.h., somewhat disappointing, but at least the highest on the journey thus far. Dauntsey was the original junction for the Marlborough branch but upon the opening of the direct line to South Wales via Badminton, a connection was made at Little Somerford during 1933 rendering the section south to Dauntsey redundant.

Six miles from Dauntsey the Chippenham stop could be made exactly to timetable, bar signal checks. The road was clear and we drew to a stop at Chippenham half a minute early. Chippenham had a locomotive depot which was a sub-shed of Swindon. It was quite large as sub-sheds go, having three roads, but on this day the occupants were just two Swindon based panniers. Chippenham was also the junction of the branch for Calne, the home of Harris meat products, which closed in September 1965.

The next stop was Bath, but we had to tackle the 1 mile 452 yard Box tunnel beforehand on another down grade of 1 in 100. It is said that the only day the sun shines through the tunnel is on April 9th, Brunel's birthday, but I have not ventured to prove this legend.

The Westbury line via Melksham at Thingley Junction, 96 miles from Paddington, flashed by and on the Box down grade SWIFT lived more up to its name and peaked at 84 m.p.h.: I had hoped for 90 plus.

At Bathampton Junction the Westbury line joined from the left and standing at the signals allowing us the right of way was a "2800" class 3819, with a rake of empty wagons.

A gentle application of the brakes and we slowed for the Bath stop, arriving two minutes early. We remained in the station for three minutes then we were off on the final leg of the journey to Bristol Temple Meads. What a magnificent stretch of urban railway the Great Western created through Bath. Much of the line is on a viaduct producing panoramic views of the City and its splendid architectural heritage.

SWIFT soon picked up speed to 70 m.p.h., which she maintained until the Bristol outskirts at St. Annes where we were briefly signal checked. From here we continued at a moderate pace until the magnificent sweep of Temple Meads station, 118 miles from Paddington, beckoned our arrival slightly ahead of schedule.

Although I had finished my journey I walked to the end of the platform to observe SWIFT departing for Weston-Super-Mare and to absorb the activity at the western end of the station. I remember one thing pleasing me greatly on this day; an arrival appearing from the Taunton direction with a "Modified Hall" pulling a 'dead' diesel with an express from the West Country.

Originally Bristol Temple Meads station consisted of two stations in one: the 1840 GWR station which was used mainly for Midland line services and the 1876 Great Western Temple Meads as we know it today, replacing an 1845 Bristol & Exeter building. The facade of Temple Meads is quite impressive with its Gothic architecture, complete with clock tower and pinnacles. The old GWR station, which is a listed building, is on the left when facing the main frontage. In 1966 the track serving the old G.W.R. station was taken up and platforms 12 to 15 closed.

Of the locomotive depots, Bath Road (82A) closed in September 1960 for conversion to a diesel traction maintenance depot to cater for the rapidly expanding ranks of diesels requiring servicing at Bristol. This of course meant a reducing number of steam hauled trains at Temple Meads.

The remaining locomotive depots in Bristol, were St. Philip's Marsh (82B) and Bristol Barrow Road (82E). The latter was formerly coded 22A, under the wing of the London Midland Region, until the regional boundaries changed. The remaining Bath Road allocation at the time of closure to steam was shared between these two depots and ultimately when St. Philip's Marsh closed the remaining allocation was transferred to Barrow Road.

During the final years of Bristol steam I paid visits to St. Philip's Marsh and Barrow Road, and a selection of photographs are included from these visits, together with a list of locomotives seen at each depot, as set out in tables 31 and 32. St. Philip's Marsh had twin round houses and a repair shop, whereas Barrow Road was a straightforward straight road shed. Of the two I found Barrow Road more atmospheric and certainly much smokier!

(opposite) **Bristol St. Philip's Marsh (82B) shed was situated on the Temple Meads avoiding line and was the principal freight locomotive shed in Bristol. The depot was closed in 1964 having served the needs of Bristol division freight for virtually 54 years. The depot consisted of two integral roundhouses and a small repair shop. Inside the shed on 25th May 1963, a trio of thoroughbreds face the turntable and from left to right are: "Modified Hall" 7907 HART HALL, "County" 1020 COUNTY OF MONMOUTH and another "Modified Hall" 6972 BENINGBROUGH HALL. All three engines were allocated to St. Philip's Marsh. Judging by the chalked train identification numbers on the boiler of 1020 she must have been the motive power for a special passenger working; the 'Z' was reserved for excursion, military or special trains running within the Western Region.**

TABLE 31. **BRISTOL ST. PHILIP'S MARSH (82B) Motive Power Depot - 26th May 1963.**

1000 Cl. 1006 COUNTY OF CORNWALL; 1010 COUNTY OF CAERNARVON; 1020 COUNTY OF MONMOUTH; 1021 COUNTY OF MONTGOMERY.
1361 Cl. 1365.
2251 Cl. 3212.
2800 Cl. 3828; 3862.
4073 Cl. 4090 DORCHESTER CASTLE; 4093 DUNSTER CASTLE; 5040 STOKESAY CASTLE; 5050 EARL OF ST. GERMANS; 5073 BLENHEIM; 5085 EVESHAM ABBEY.
4300 Cl. 6312; 6320; 7338.
4700 Cl. 4700.
4900 Cl. 4922 ENVILLE HALL; 4947 NANHORAN HALL; 4949 PACKWOOD HALL; 4960 PYLE HALL; 4991 COBHAM HALL; 4992 CROSBY HALL; 4993 DALTON HALL; 4996 EDEN HALL; 4999 GOPSAL HALL; 5900 HINDERTON HALL; 5904 KELHAM HALL; 5934 KNELLER HALL; 5940 WHITBOURNE HALL; 5958 KNOLTON HALL; 6912 HELMSTER HALL; 6954 LOTHERTON HALL; 6958 OXBURGH HALL.
5101 Cl. 4102.
5700 Cl. 3623; 6769; 9601; 9729.
6400 Cl. 6408.
6800 Cl. 6813 EASTBURY GRANGE; 6814 ENBOURNE GRANGE; 6846 RUCKLEY GRANGE; 6873 CARADOC GRANGE.
6959 Cl. 6972 BENINGBROUGH HALL; 6981 MARBURY HALL; 7901 DODINGTON HALL; 7907 HART HALL; 7911 LADY MARGARET HALL; 7916 MOBBERLEY HALL; 7924 THORNEYCROFT HALL; 7927 WILLINGTON HALL.
7800 Cl. 7805 BROOME MANOR.
Cl. 4F 44102.
Cl. WD 90237.
Cl. 9F 92208.
Total : 57

This was indeed a pleasant sight to see; an ex-works "Hall" standing outside St. Philip's Marsh shed. No.6958 OXBURGH HALL had no doubt worked up from Swindon before going to its home depot at Pontypool Road (86G), which was some ten miles north of Newport on the Hereford route.

On the south side of St. Philip's Marsh shed, on 25th May 1963, stood a line of withdrawn engines which included 2-8-0 No.4700 and Pannier 3623. The "4700" would never steam again as the piston rod and cylinder cover have been removed presumably to make dead engine movement easier. Close buffered to the two engines are the tenders of a pair of "Halls", also withdrawn - 4960 PYLE HALL and 5940 WHITBOURNE HALL.

My final photograph at St. Philip's Marsh depicts the only Midland Railway designed engine on shed: "4F" 44102. The engine was however allocated within Western Region territory at Templecombe (82G) and appears to be in store. The evidence suggesting this is the rather tatty sacking draped over the chimney. Ex-WD Austerity 2-8-0 No.90237 from Woodford Halse shed (2F) stands in steam next to the "4F".

TABLE 32. **BRISTOL BARROW ROAD (82E)**
Motive Power Depot - May 1963.

2251 Cl.   2217; 2277; 3218.
5101 Cl.   4103; 4131.
5700 Cl.   3632; 3643; 3675; 3677; 3702; 3758; 3795; 4619;
4699; 5765; 8752; 9623; 9626.
6100 Cl.   6147; 6148.
8100 Cl.   8102.
Cl. 2   41207; 41208; 41245; 41248; 41249; 41304.
Cl. 4F   43924.
Cl. 4F   44209; 44264; 44269; 44523; 44580; 44584.
Cl. 5   44853; 44858.
Cl. 6P5F   45682 TRAFALGAR; 45685 BARFLEUR.
Cl. 7P   46120 ROYAL INNISKILLING FUSILIER.
Cl. 3F   47557.
Cl. 8F   48101; 48109; 48303; 48431.
Cl. 3   82007; 82035; 82037; 82038; 82039; 82040; 82043.
Cl. 4   75001.
Cl. 5   73015; 73028; 73047.
Cl. 9F   92000; 92007; 92008; 92138; 92157; 92221.

Total : 61

(below) **This is one of my personal favourite shed scenes. It was taken at Bristol Barrow Road shed (82E), formally a Midland depot coded 22A, on 25th May 1963. Stanier 8F 48101 rests awhile as the crew take a break sharing conversation with their mates, all oblivious of the taking of this little slice of a 1960's railway working day.**

(below) **Midland "4F" 44580, with a full tender of coal, simmers at the side of the Barrow Road roundhouse waiting for its next scheduled duty. On the day this photograph was taken there were no less than sixteen different classes of locomotives present on shed ranging from Western 'Panniers' to a LM 'Royal Scot' locomotive.**

Next stop Bridgend for "Castle" 5048 EARL OF DEVON, photographed west of Llanharen, with a Paddington to Pembroke Dock express on 28th July 1962. The photograph was taken whilst I was on a summer holiday spent with my relations. During trips out in the car a break was spent, whenever possible, by the side of a railway line. On this occasion I had hoped for a "7200" tank to pass with a freight, but it fell upon "2800" Class 2861, travelling smartly on the heels of 5048, to provide the final steam contentment of the day.

The impending end of steam is evident in this view of Cardiff East Dock shed yard, photographed in the final year of Western steam in 1965. The shed sidings are littered with redundant "5600", "5700" and "9400" Class tanks. The large locomotive shed was empty and the only engine standing in steam and ready for action was "9F" 92244. This was to be one of the most miserable scenes that I witnessed during the final run down of steam.

8: SOUTH WALES - THE LAND OF THE RED DRAGON

Wales is the land of the mythical Red Dragon and it was fitting in the halcyon days of steam to name one of the Paddington to South Wales expresses accordingly. The down train left Paddington for Carmarthen at 5.55 p.m. and the up working, which in 1962, left Carmarthen at 7.15 a.m. arrived in London at 12.55 p.m. Other prestigious Welsh expresses were named *THE PEMBROKE COAST EXPRESS*, *THE SOUTH WALES PULLMAN* and *THE CAPITALS UNITED EXPRESS* which complimented the ensemble of trains forming the regular interval hourly service between London and South Wales, in the main departing at five minutes to each hour.

The Welsh expresses were heavily patronised both by business people and the Welsh population of the south-east, who had moved to London and the home counties in search of work during 'The Great Depression'. It was difficult to find travelling space in the height of summer, as standing room only forced passengers to use their cases as seats in the narrow corridors of the twelve coach or so formation.

No matter what the loading of these expresses, the "Castles" and "Britannia's" proved their worth as they forged onward through Swindon, the Severn tunnel, Newport, into Cardiff and beyond. These magnificent engines were allocated to either Old Oak Common, Cardiff Canton or Landore for these top link duties. In the early sixties, following the displacement of the "Kings" from the West of England, they too saw service into Cardiff, albeit briefly before the "Western" class diesel-hydraulics sounded the death knell for main line steam into South Wales.

The closure of Landore shed to steam in 1961, to commence conversion into a modern diesel maintenance and servicing depot, to cater for the new "Western" arrivals, caused the remaining steam motive power to be transferred to Neath. Up to that time Neath had seen little evidence of express passenger types in its two roundhouses.

Landore steam shed served the Swansea area with its passenger motive power, that is excluding the Central Wales line into Swansea (Victoria), which had its own motive power depot close to the station of London & North Western origin. The locomotives backed down to Swansea (High Street) station for both eastbound trains to Cardiff and beyond and westbound for Carmarthen and Pembrokeshire. It was possible to experience a variety of motive power on a journey between Paddington and Pembroke Dock, with reversal of direction at both the Swansea and Carmarthen stops, and a possible engine change at Cardiff. The sequence of changes may have involved a change from a "Britannia" at Cardiff to a "Castle" between Cardiff and Swansea, a "Hall" to Carmarthen and finally the journey may have ended with a "4300" Mogul in charge of a formation that had been reduced in size following the removal of the restaurant facilities at Swansea.

It was a pleasing experience to observe Neyland allocated Mogul 5357 with a *PEMBROKE COAST EXPRESS* headboard being fitted on its smokebox door lamp bracket in Carmarthen station, ready to haul the express on the final stage of its journey to Pembroke Dock. Other larger types of locomotives were used west of Carmarthen, notably "Counties" and "Halls", allocated to Neyland and Goodwick, which would sometimes run through to Cardiff on parcels or Fishguard Harbour boat trains, missing reversal stops at Swansea and Carmarthen. Normally an engine from the far west of Pembrokeshire

I must confess to be very fond of this view looking towards Aberdare station (visible in the distance) taken on 30th July 1962. Despite all the signals showing danger there is a sense of activity far removed from the present day scene at Aberdare. 5698 restarts a train of coal empties bound for Glyn Neath after a signal check. Standing on an adjacent track "4200" Class 5258 pauses after marshalling its train. In the yard a pannier shunts coal wagons and on the far left a short rake of passenger coaches waits to be collected by yet another tank engine, to form a train to Pontypool Road. Aberdare locomotive shed is out of view to the left of the siding containing coaches.

In June 1964 the connection between Aberdare and Pontypool Road, which traversed the impressive structure of Crumlin Viaduct, was severed. Two years before closure of the line "5600" Class 5624 draws away from Aberdare (High Level) with a stopping train for Pontypool Road. Aberdare boasted two stations, that depicted in the photograph at High Level with through trains between Pontypool Road, Neath and Swansea High Street. The other was the Low Level station with auto trains to Abercynon and rush hour trains to Pontypridd and Cardiff. In recent times, after many years without passenger trains, Aberdare once more has a train service to Cardiff and beyond, following a resurgence of passenger traffic in the Welsh Valleys.

would not travel further than Cardiff where a change was made for the remainder of the journey. I may of course stand corrected!

There was never a dull moment at Cardiff (General) when steam was king. The up centre through road was seldom without a freight held at the lights. The green aspect beckoned them on one by one, down the grade and under the connecting line to the Taff Vale and Cardiff (Queen Street) station. A large proportion of the freight was coal and metal traffic, invariably hauled by "4200" or "7200" heavy freight tanks.

Much of the freight in South Wales emanated from either the Cardiff and Newport valleys, the steel works on the Bristol Channel coastline or the docks at Newport, Cardiff, Barry and Swansea. Each dock system had a motive power depot close by, with a varied assortment of motive power suitable for working the tangle of tracks. Swansea docks boasted two locomotive depots, one at Danygraig and the other at East Dock. I remember the contrast between the two depots: the former appeared quite respectable and tidy, but the latter was dingy and created an atmosphere full of hanging smoke. At least, these are my experiences.

The volume of freight generated by and for the South Wales industries necessitated marshalling yards to sort the traffic into appropriate train loads. Severn Tunnel Junction was the principal marshalling yard for South Wales. There was always intense activity in its miles of sidings, with wagons rolling down the humps, being

sorted into train loads with a clang of buffers as each wagon met another. The sounds constantly repeating as the slack on each train load was taken up, only to bounce apart to tension the couplings ready for the next impact.

The yard was serviced by Severn Tunnel Junction locomotive shed, remembered by its post nationalisation coding of 86E. In addition to the freight activity, the shed was responsible for banking trains through the Severn tunnel as far as Pilning on the opposite side of the Severn estuary. In 1986 it was announced that Severn Tunnel Junction yard would close. Now those sidings have been lifted, leaving the land to return to nature. Slowly the system shrinks back to meet the ever changing operational pattern, block train loads of freight from point to point, a reduction in the number of operating coal mines and disuse of the docks.

In the Welsh Valleys the abundance of 'black gold' that was coal created the mining communities, where houses still cling to the mountain-sides in terraced ribbons of locally quarried stone, dusky with time. Above the housing line, quarry scars pepper the mountain-side with bare rock and stunted trees with roots that cling to rock overhangs preserving their co-existence.

On the floor of the valleys collieries once flourished, serving each community with industry and jobs with dampness and darkness as ever present companions. The wheels of each pit winding gear taking men down to work the coal face and bringing dram loads of

0-6-2T 5698 with a 'shunters dummy' takes the connecting line between Aberdare (High Level) and Low Level stations on 3rd October 1962. In 1958 over 75 per cent of the 200 members of the "5600" Class were allocated to depots within South Wales, west of Severn Tunnel Junction.

coal to the surface to fill the waiting wagons at the pit head. Everywhere was coal dust, which washed into the rivers that once carved the landscape turning them black, destroying the aquatic life.

The sound of the pit sirens ending each shift heralded the sound of the boots of men trudging homeward to remove the thick layer of grime that covered their bodies from head to toe. Shunting sounds echoed through the valley as 'panniers' and "5600" tank engines worked the pit sidings replacing full wagons with a fresh supply of empties. The largest mines had their own industrial motive power to convey the loaded coal wagons to the reception sidings and return empties to the pit head.

One by one the pits have closed, leaving the skeletal remains of buildings with window panes smashed into jagged remnants and insecure corrugated metal cladding rattling in the wind. The pit sidings oxidise on cracked and rotting sleepers, points seize up with the passage of time and lack of lubrication and weeds struggle to colonise the black earth of the waste land. Soon the bulldozers demolish the buildings, the rubble filling redundant pit shafts. The sidings are lifted, the black landscape levelled and grass planted to form recreational areas and opportunities created for new industry in an attempt to keep the life blood of each community flowing. Only the slag heaps remain as a reminder of the valleys industrial past, but here too the slag may be used for road building material, or the heap may be landscaped and taken over by the forestry. The once black rivers flow clear as crystal and water life returns once more, and those railways that have survived the loss of freight revenue meander through a new rural landscape.

The Rhondda, at the height of coal production in South Wales, had pits at every twist and turn of both valleys. Maerdy at the head

of the Rhondda Fach was the last pit in the Rhondda, but sadly that too has succumbed to uneconomic extraction and has been demolished and filled in leaving the rails of the Porth to Maerdy branch to join the many other railway redundancies.

Maerdy was one of the last pits in Wales where industrial steam could be seen operational, that is when the diesel shunter had failed or was being serviced. I recall two steam engines at Maerdy, ex-GWR pannier 9792, which I never saw operational, and a large Pecket saddletank 2150. It was a magnificent spectacle to see the Pecket puffing clouds of steam into the mountain air as it moved empties along the impossibly uneven track from the reception sidings to the pit.

Although coal was the dominant reason for the existence of the valley railways in Wales, as the communities grew with the emergence of mining, passenger traffic played an ever increasing role in the pattern of services. Prior to the introduction of diesel multiple units, motive power was invariably "5600" class tanks for the longer distance local traffic and "4500" and "6400" classes were used on the shorter branch trains. I remember travelling between Porth and Cardiff with 5617 in charge of a rake of six suburban coaches. After the Radyr stop speed gathered until it approached 70 m.p.h. through the suburbs of Cardiff. The speed was ascertained by a rail joint count compared to time, a well tried and tested method used by rail enthusiasts of the period. This was prior to the days of long welded rails which removed the familiar 'clickety-clack' sound. Calculations, however, could easily be totally confused when the train travelled over a series of points.

The "5600" tank only had 4' 7½" driving wheels, consequently high speed behind one of these engines was quite an experience. It

NEATH DISTRICT - 30th July 1959

Table 33: **NEATH (87A)**

1600 Cl. 1645.
4100 Cl. 4169; 5102.
4200 Cl. 4242; 4264; 4281; 4284; 4288; 5222; 5246.
5600 Cl. 5656.
5700 Cl. 3611; 3621; 7701; 7743; 7757; 8782; 9627; 9779; 9786.
6800 Cl. 6878 LONGFORD GRANGE.
8100 Cl. 8104.
9400 Cl. 8445; 8452; 9446; 9448; 9478.

Total : 27.

Table 34: **NEATH N&B (Sub shed of 87A)**

5700 Cl. 3757; 4621.

Total : 2.

Table 35: **DUFFRYN YARD (87B)**

4200 Cl. 4278; 4296; 5205; 5216; 5220; 5221.
5600 Cl. 5604; 6602; 6620; 6662.
5700 Cl. 3613; 3781; 3791; 4681; 4684; 4695; 5738; 5770; 6725; 6761; 9634; 9736; 9742; 9766; 9785; 9799.
7200 Cl. 7249.
9400 Cl. 8407; 8490; 9456; 9457.

Total : 31.

Table 36: **DANYGRAIG (87C)**

1101 Cl. 1101; 1104.
S.H.T. 1145.
1600 Cl. 1640; 1647.
4200 Cl. 4232; 5210; 5211; 5232; 5261.
4300 Cl. 7340.
5600 Cl. 6686.
5700 Cl. 3633; 3679; 4666; 4694; 5704; 5731; 6719; 6762; 6766; 7793; 8731; 8738; 9794.
7200 Cl. 7221; 7226; 7248.
7400 Cl. 7402; 7439.
9400 Cl. 8416.

Total : 31.

Table 37: **SWANSEA EAST DOCK (87D)**

S.H.T. 1144.
1600 Cl. 1641.
5700 Cl. 3641; 7704; 7756.

Total : 5.

NEATH DISTRICT - SUNDAY IN AUGUST 1961

Table 38: **NEATH (87A)**

P & M. 1152.
1600 Cl. 1645.
2800 Cl. 3848.
4073 Cl. WINDSOR CASTLE; 4093 DUNSTER CASTLE; 5013 ABERGAVENNY CASTLE; 5021 WHITTINGTON CASTLE; 5036 LYONSHALL CASTLE; 5037 MONMOUTH CASTLE; 5041 TIVERTON CASTLE; 5048 EARL OF DEVON; 5051 EARL BATHURST; 5074 HAMPDEN; 7017 G.J.CHURCHWARD.
4200 Cl. 4282; 4284; 5221; 5233; 5242.
4900 Cl. 4927 FARNBOROUGH HALL; 5989 CRANSLEY HALL; 6905 CLAUGHTON HALL; 6918 SANDON HALL.
5600 Cl. 5670; 5673; 6641; 6649; 6695.
5700 Cl. 3621; 3637; 3766; 3768; 3774; 4621; 4653; 5761; 5773; 5778; 8732; 8749; 8775; 8788; 9779; 9792.
6959 Cl. 6961 STEDHAM HALL.
7200 Cl. 7204; 7247; 7249.
7800 Cl. 7805 BROOME MANOR.
8100 Cl. 8102; 8104.
9400 Cl. 9412; 9442; 9446; 9448; 9452; 9473; 9478.
Cl. 8F 48461.
Cl. 7P6F 70027 RISING STAR.
Shunter D3429.

Total : 61.

Three of the above locomotives: 1152; 3766 and 8104 were labelled "STORE AT DANYGRAIG", despite the fact that Danygraig depot was closed to steam. The pre-grouping owner of 1152 was Powlesland & Mason (Contractor), P & M in the table.

Table 39: **DUFFRYN YARD (87B)**

4200 Cl. 4213; 4230; 4256; 4270; 4278; 4286; 4289; 4296; 4299; 5203; 5216; 5224; 5232; 5246; 5254; 5262.
4300 Cl. 7306.
5600 Cl. 5604; 6620; 6686.
5700 Cl. 3613; 3642; 3688; 3692; 3718; 3762; 3791; 4695; 5728; 5770; 5787; 8724; 8772; 9617; 9634; 9671; 9715; 9742; 9766; 9785; 9799.
9400 Cl. 8407; 8416; 8482; 8490; 9454; 9456; 9457; 9483.

Total : 49.

(opposite, top) **Pannier tanks photographed at the side of Abercynon shed (88E) on 30th July 1962. Included are 9723 and 8730. On that day the following engines were present at the depot: 1612; 1641; 3603; 3707; 3734; 5630; 5647; 5657; 5699; 8730; 9723; 9728.**

(opposite, bottom) **The "5600" Class tanks were stalwarts of the Welsh Valleys. Here 5657 rests at Abercynon, sandwiched between two "Panniers" one of which had just buffered up to the rear on 30th July 1962. This shed was closed in 1964 after thirty-five years of servicing engines for duties in the Taff Vale, having replaced an earlier Taff Vale Railway depot situated on the same site.**

Following the demise of steam, "Hymeks" were common motive power on express passenger work. Here D7028 pauses at Cardiff (General) with a passenger turn to Swansea in July 1963. In my youth many holidays were spent with my relations in the Rhondda Valley. I was soon to discover the weekly rover ticket that allowed unlimited travel over a large area of Glamorgan. In consequence many hours were spent on Cardiff (General) watching the endless procession of freight passing through the station. This was in my pre-photographic recording days when the numbers were of paramount importance in my attempts to see everything. Although I could only manage a brief spell of photography on the station during that summer day in 1963, I was able to capture one steam photograph, but upon printing the negative a large black post appeared out of the chimney and in consequence I have excluded it from this collection. It is interesting to note that the engine was Pannier 9723, ex-works, with an 81C (Southall) shed plate. Upon checking the list of locomotives repaired at Caerphilly this particular engine appears, and thus offers an explanation.

could be likened to a "2800" freight on an express, a combination that was not unknown at the height of the Summer Saturday holiday traffic in Devon, when everything available was pressed into service.

For a time Swindon built "82000" series BR Standard tanks were used on the Treherbet to Barry Island services but by the early sixties steam had been replaced on the valley passenger services by diesel multiple units. This was to be a different experience particularly in the front seats observing the driver take the meandering bends muffling the ATC siren with his hand when approaching an horizontal distant semaphore. The most rewarding experience was to observe the steam hauled oncoming freight traffic and the occupants of the goods yards as they flashed by.

It is interesting to recall a journey between Tylorstown, on the Porth to Maerdy branch, and Cardiff (General) shortly after the introduction of diesel multiple units on the majority of the valley services. The rail journey to Porth from Tylorstown only took eight minutes or so. It was preferable to catching the Rhondda bus since the branch arrival times in Porth were arranged to connect with the Treherbet to Barry Island service. I remember being disappointed as a multiple unit entered the station in place of a "4500" tank and its two auto-coaches. It was double track to Porth, with an intermediate station at Ynyshir, and as the d.m.u. rounded the bend through Wattstown, 5693 trundled past with a short train of empty coal wagons. A lowered semaphore beckoned my train into Porth station where it slowed to a halt on the island platform.

Only a few minutes passed before the connection to Cardiff and Barry arrived. In the height of summer the Barry Island trains were brim full with day trippers to the seaside, but on this day there were plenty of seats available because rain had been forecast. With luck a front seat was empty and duly occupied. A buzz from the guard and the train moved off facing all clear semaphores into Pontypridd. Trehafod is midway between Porth and Pontypridd and shortly after the station the up line semaphore lowered to herald a bunker first "9400" class pannier with a single "toad" guards van.

Pontypridd was a major junction of the Taff Vale Railway where the Merthyr line joined in a multiple of cross-overs just north of the station. Waiting for the road on the goods line was 6607, with a long rake of coal empties. Pontypridd goods yard was out of view around the Merthyr curve but, no doubt, a "1600" pannier from Abercynon shed was busily at work.

Following the Treforest stop we were rounding the sweeping bends towards Taffs Well on the four track section. An oncoming freight appeared with 5676 hard on the heels of the 'empties' occupying the Pontypridd loop. As the guards van passed by, the rear of another came into view on the down goods line. A fully laden coal train, with 6699 in charge, was quickly overtaken. She was sending out a good smoke screen which temporarily obscured the forward view from the d.m.u. Little notice was taken of oncoming multiple units, but the driver gave a wave of recognition as they rumbled past. At Taffs Well, the Nantgarw colliery branch joined the Taff Vale

On the same day another "Hymek" D7037 waits to restart a train to Paddington which I believe to be the 11.10 a.m. from Milford Haven. Not a single member of the 101 strong "Hymek" class ever carried a name. This was presumably due to a policy of not naming any engine under Type 4 status. This policy is certainly not adopted today when any engine from a shunter to a Class 60 could be endowed with a personal identity. I made a return visit to Cardiff (General) for a three hour stint of photography during May 1991. The traction scene had changed dramatically: freight were ever present albeit in lesser numbers, but the passenger turns were exclusively in the hands of HST's, sprinter units or the older style multiple units during the time spent in observation.

shortly before the Rhymney line to Caerphilly via Nantgarw Bank also joined our route. Shortly after Taffs Well station the train passed under Cherry Tree viaduct which carried the Rhymney branch of the Barry Railway.

At Radyr a hive of shunting activity was evident with panniers of "5700" and "9400" classes sorting wagons in the yard. Radyr shed was tucked away at the rear of the complex and showed signs of smoke and steam mingling into the misty atmosphere of a damp Welsh morning. Not a tender engine in sight until the d.m.u. dropped down from Queen Street station over the ex-GWR main line and into General station. Here a "Castle" and a "Grange" were waiting for their respective paths toward Newport, Severn tunnel and England.

South Wales is littered with the remains of railway lines that once provided journeys similar to that described. Fortunately the Treherbet to Barry line still remains. Some of the less fortunate centres of population have been severed from the rail network completely. Brecon could once be reached from Newport, Neath, Moat Lane and Hereford. Now only the track beds remain to serve as a reminder of these picturesque rural railways that were doomed by the Beeching cuts.

Walking along the trackbed of the Brecon & Merthyr Railway, which in some places has been converted into a National Park footpath, one imagines the lost potential for tourism that these railways could have generated, as the more remoter parts of the principality are promoted through conservation and heritage campaigns. To some extent this has been offset by the construction of the Brecon Mountain Railway on the trackbed of the former B&MR between Pontsticill Junction and Pant.

Further south, into Glamorgan, the intensity of closed railway's rapidly increases with perhaps the most significant being the route

between Neath and Pontypool Road, although small sections still exist, notably at Aberdare. The line traversed the Ebbw valley by means of the magnificent Crumlin viaduct. I regret not taking photographs of this structure with its iron lattice trestles reaching from the valley floor to the dizzy height of 60 metres. What a breathtaking experience it must have been easing a passenger train over the trestles with a "4100" class tank leading a formation of six coaches. Both the viaduct and the Aberdare to Pontypool Road train are lost forever - only memories remain.

Steam locomotives still existed in South Wales as recently as 1989, but their fires had long since been dropped and the passage of time scarred their remains. The salty atmosphere of the scrap yard in Barry docks rendered the engines into severely corroded hulks, the home of wasteland colonising plants where only the butterfly reflected the resplendent livery that was once worn by these majestic beasts of man's making. Yet all are now removed by preservation bodies intent on returning them to their former splendour; a formidable task.

In *tables 33-39* on page 74, are records of visits made to the Neath District locomotive depots in July 1959 and again in August 1961. It is interesting to note that the occupants of Neath (87A) grew considerably in 1961 following the closure of Landore (87E) motive power depot for conversion into a diesel depot.

The locomotives from Landore were divided between Neath and Llanelly (87F), which resulted in Neath depot having a variety of types hitherto rarely seen on that depot. The comparison between the two visit records clearly indicate this. The visit of July 1959 was the culmination of the cycle ride to Wales mentioned in the introduction.

Standard Class 4 mixed traffic locomotive 75020, a Machynlleth engine, was photographed in very dismal weather conditions on 15th December 1962 at Carmarthen. The engine had just arrived with a train from Aberystwyth.

I was unable to resist including this scene of NCB owned Pecket tank No. 2150 shunting at the Maerdy Colliery exchange sidings on 8th October 1975. The normal diesel shunter used for this duty had been broken down for six weeks and the steam standby had to be brought to life for a spell of duty. The driver was interested in my photography and invited me into the cab for a chat during his tea break. How the engine stayed on the tracks with the severe irregularities both at the rail joints and in the subsided track bed I will never know. Alas this scene is no more. The track has all been lifted and the colliery, a little distance further into the head of the valley, has been totally flattened and obliterated. In May, 1991 the track of the Maerdy branch as far as the site of Maerdy station was still *in situ*, albeit rusting and becoming overgrown, but I noticed that it had been lifted when passing the mine site in December 1995. The redundant trackbed between Porth and Maerdy would make a marvellous standard or narrow gauge tourist railway, as the valley floor from Tylorstown to the head of the valley is very picturesque.

"Western" diesel hydraulic, **1021 WESTERN CAVALIER**, powers through Undy near Severn Tunnel Junction on 24th April 1973. Judging by the Z in the headcode panel, the train is a special working. The outer tracks are the freight lines which remain in this position as far as Llanwern steel works. After the steel works both slow lines are situated to the left of the mainline (facing Newport).

I have included this photograph in the collection because "9F" **92085** was one of two engines cut up at Barry in 1980, the other being **4156**. However one cannot complain in view of the very large number of engines rescued from the cutters torch. Locomotives present at Barry and their fate or rescue into preservation is well documented in the Railway press and space precludes detailed information.

(*above*) **Denham station on a sunny spring Saturday morning in 1961 has more staff than passengers waiting for the arrival of 42588 with a Marylebone suburban train. The through centre tracks at Denham allowed fast running for the Wolverhampton and Birkenhead expresses and speeds in excess of 90 m.p.h. were not uncommon. In 1958 Neasden depot was coded 14D in London Midland territory having previously reported to the Eastern Region as 34E. 42588 carries a 14D shedplate having been transferred to Neasden upon territory changes.**

(*left*) **The view from the down platform at Denham station, looking towards Denham Golf Club in 1961. The down platform loop is set for an Aylesbury local and the up main beckons a freight from Woodford Halse.**

9: NORTH TO SHREWSBURY VIA THE GW&GC JOINT

For volume of traffic the Great Western and Great Central Joint line through High Wycombe was a poor relation to the Western Region main line through Reading. Nevertheless it had its own unique character and certainly a more varied compliment of motive power. Memories of this route through Buckinghamshire and onward to Birmingham Snow Hill, Wolverhampton Low Level and Shrewsbury are full of nostalgic reflections of the workings of Eastern, Midland and BR Standard design engines amidst the flow of traffic between Paddington and destinations to Birkenhead and North Wales.

The height of a trainspotters fulfilment was to observe a 6C Birkenhead allocated "Grange" in the London division. The names that linger in my memory of two such examples were Yiewsley and Marlas Grange, but I have no tale to tell of their siting during their stay at "6C" south of Banbury on the GW/GC Joint, but I remember seeing both engines on freight at Iver.

The nearest location for traffic observation and photography to my home in Iver was Denham. Many Saturday morning experiences were enjoyed at this station together with those at West Ruislip and Denham Golf Club, the next stations on the line travelling up and down respectively.

Being allowed on Denham station was an enthusiasts privilege and it was prudent to ask permission since the down line platform waiting room was well desecrated with graffiti, both with regard to spotters observations and adolescent fondness for the opposite sex. The staff's attention to the environment tidiness was both obvious and understandable. Scribed comments regarding observations of "A3's" or "WD" 90002 on freshly painted walls was severely frowned upon. Not to mention rhymes containing words not found in the English dictionary!

My first visit to Denham was for the sole purpose of seeing "Castle" 5047 EARL OF DARTMOUTH, which for reasons only known to Wolverhampton Stafford Road locomotive department was an extremely rare visitor to the Reading main line, despite regular sitings of its sister engines similarly allocated. Rumour suggested that a Saturday morning at Denham would turn up trumps for a siting of 5047 on an up Wolverhampton to Paddington express.

Denham was a cold place being situated on an embankment on the down grade from Gerrards Cross. The winter winds chilled the fingers and the use of the waiting room was greatly appreciated to record observations. In warmer weather standing outside the platform situated signal box was a rewarding experience listening for the call attention bell and the subsequent bell codings identifying forthcoming traffic.

On "Earl of Dartmouth" day it was a cold blustery Autumn morning prior to the dawn of the 1960's and accelerating modernisation. It was the close of the "L1" era on the High Wycombe and Aylesbury local traffic. Their shrill whistles unmistakably identifying the class as each driver opened the regulator to ease the train out of the platform loop to join the double track into the Chilterns. In November 1957, Neasden had seventeen members of this class providing an impressionable Eastern flavour to this ex-Great Western and Great Central Joint line. However, within a short space of time all were to be transferred away to be replaced with Midland "4MT" tanks some of which, together with "80000" series Standard tanks, were already sharing the services with the "L1's".

Having sought permission to spend the morning on the down platform it was necessary to negotiate the damp and draughty subway.

I remember the wind whistling through the subway as I briskly climbed the steps to the platform (on a more recent visit, little seems to have changed!). During the transit from up to down platform, the up platform loop lower quadrant signal had lowered heralding the approach of wheezing 67769 with a Marylebone bound local. A shrill burst of the apparently mandatory whistle and she was off to the next port of call at West Ruislip (renamed from Ruislip and Ickenham). A short time later the down through road was given the all clear for the 9.10 a.m. to Birkenhead. On this day 6001 KING EDWARD VII showed a good head of steam as she pounded through with every carriage window full of faces identifying their progress by the station sign stating that this was Denham for Harefield. The steam lingered a while under the station awning until a fresh gust of wind evacuated all trace into the cold October air.

There were many quiet spells at Denham but there were busy periods as well, particularly when the yard was shunted by a "6100" tank simultaneously as a local was held in the station loop for an express to pass through.

The morning progressed with locals, all with "L1's" in charge, spiced with "Kings" on express traffic and a "WD" 2-8-0 from Woodford Halse shed on an up freight. A lengthy dull spell followed, to be broken with the resounding clang of the up main semaphore bouncing into the off position which caused the sparrows perched on the arm to scatter in mild panic. Within seconds the platform loop was also cleared for a down local and I remember hoping that the stopper would not obscure my view of the up train and the possibility of EARL OF DARTMOUTH passing unidentified. Good fortune prevailed as the beats of a Collett exhaust, clearly audible heading down the grade through Denham Golf Club, preceding the siting of the down stopper.

It was feasible for high speeds through Denham and I was later, in 1964, to experience 94 m.p.h. through the station behind two-tone green Brush diesel D1710, which along with a down run on the same day with another Brush, D1682, are shown in *tables 45* and *46*. But, back to that cold October morning.

As the engine came into view she was clearly a "Castle" going fast and easy. Anticipation mounted as the train neared. There were no reporting numbers on the engine's smoke box door and I strained my eyes for the smoke box number. 5047 rapidly came into focus and within seconds a very clean EARL OF DARTMOUTH thundered through the station, the relatively small amount of steam briefly obscuring my view of the carriages before the signal returned to its horizontal resting position within moments of its passing. The clatter of carriages quickly diminished as 5047 dissolved into the distance. Silence prevailed until the sparrows plucked up enough courage to regain their perch on the horizontal signal arm, chirping to their companions in the process.

In all my years of railway observation I was never to see EARL OF DARTMOUTH at any other location on the Region, but I did return to Denham for a repeat performance on a number of occasions. As luck would have it by the time the photographic bug took hold, her schedule must have changed on the days of my visits for I never saw her again.

On another occasion I attempted to photograph the last run of 6018 KING HENRY VI at Denham but she was going too fast to achieve an acceptable result, swaying gently from side to side as she rattled through.

Not only does EARL OF DARTMOUTH linger in my memory (I seem to remember long ago railway events more readily than having to get carrots from the greengrocer!), but the first time that I had ever seen an "A3" was at Denham. The precise date eludes me but it was a Saturday in the mid nineteen-fifties. The time I do recall, about 12.50 p.m., past the hour I should have been cycling home for my dinner, but the time honoured practice of waiting for one more signal to drop prevailed.

A down train on the through road was 'pegged', though not at the right time for a Paddington departure. Perhaps a freight or something unexpected? The latter category proved to be correct as an unfamiliar shape loomed closer under a powerful head of steam. The engine was 60059 TRACERY which I later established to be the 12.15 p.m. Marylebone to Manchester express which used the GW&GC Joint instead of the direct route via Harrow used by the 10 a.m. and 3.20 p.m. departures.

I had discovered that the Great Western locomotives had some competition in both design and elegance. On later visits I managed to observe one other member of the class, 60049 GALTEE MORE, on this turn until the timetable altered the arrangements. Excursions to Kings Cross were necessary to experience the full flavour of 'Eastern promise'.

Two other Eastern sightings before the dawn of the sixties remain firmly implanted in my memory: a York based "B16", 61419, on a freight, which I saw from an overbridge at South Harefield, and "V2" 60847 ST.PETERS SCHOOL YORK A.D.627. on the same stretch of line.

It is strange how unimportant experiences can also linger in ones memory. I can only have been five or six years old when I remember trying to jump from sleeper to sleeper along the little used Uxbridge (High Street) branch during an after dinner walk with my parents, long before I had any interest in railways. The derelict Uxbridge (High Street) station comes to mind; perched on the beginnings of a viaduct, stunted before it traversed the old A40 road, the original intention was to connect with Uxbridge (Vine Street) but this never materialised.

At the time of my visits to Denham, the Uxbridge branch was used for freight only, the passenger services being axed before the Second World War. During the conflict the branch was lifted for 'war effort' material and re-laid again at the end of hostilities. In its final years of operation "4500" class tanks transferred into the London division from the remoter parts of the region were frequently used on the Denham branch goods.

There was one day each year when a visit to the GW&GC Joint was irresistible no matter what the weather: the Football Association Cup Final day. The progress of the two teams were monitored through to the final, not for the purposes of following a favourite club, although at this point I must confess a slight fondness for Manchester United, but to hope for two teams in the final hailing from the Midlands or the North. This was certain to result in a flow of extra trains to Wembley, some of which would use the Joint line, and others, the busy Euston main line.

My first experience of this procession was on 7th May 1960, following a tip-off from a fellow enthusiast who had travelled to Iver for a spell of trainspotting from Denham. On this day Wolves and Blackburn were in the final, a certain combination for an interesting mornings observation.

I chose the up platform of Denham Golf Club to observe the specials. The traffic was heavy with five specials before 1.00 p.m. from each of the two clubs. The Wolverhampton trains were all hauled by Western Region 4-6-0's and those from Blackburn all Eastern Region engines: *Table 40* records the observations.

On another occasion in 1964, when Preston were in the final, three "Britannia's" were used: 70000 BRITANNIA, 70050 FIRTH OF CLYDE, and 70052 FIRTH OF TAY. The latter pair had spent most of their working life on the Scottish Region, appropriately named to register that fact.

All three locomotives were very grimy but still appeared to be in reasonable shape, going well with heavy loads. A few years earlier the two Scottish "Brits" would indeed have been a rare sight this far south of the border.

On my last Cup Final day pilgrimage, in 1965 and this time to West Ruislip, every special was, much to my disappointment, diesel hauled. The steady procession on the centre through road, nevertheless, brought a variety of motive power to the line. "Peak's" D16 and D18, Class "40's" D303 and D310, as well as three or more Class "47's".

This diesel take-over caused my attention to be centred elsewhere in the search for steam. The green diesels of the time would, however, have drawn a large following in today's railway scene. A short two hour stay at Seer Green on 20th April 1965, recorded in *Table 41*, shows diesels were very evident in the closing years of steam on this line.

The Birkenhead line from Paddington was on the very fringe of Western territory which accounted for the great variety of motive power to be seen prior to the lifting of the Great Central route from

---

TABLE 40. **DENHAM GOLF CLUB - Saturday 7th MAY 1960. CUP FINAL SPECIALS - WOLVES AND BLACKBURN**

Time	Loco.	Name	Depot	Reporting No.	Team
9.56 a.m.	5930	HANNINGTON HALL	84F	X21	Wolves
10.39	6022	KING EDWARD III	84A	X22	Wolves
10.54	6014	KING HENRY VII	84A	X23	Wolves
11.03	60950	—	50A	C850	Blackburn
11.11	5045	EARL OF DUDLEY	84A	X24	Wolves
11.35	61169	—	41A	C851	Blackburn
11.50	60863	—	15E	C852	Blackburn
11.57	7922	SALFORD HALL	84G	X25	Wolves
12.15 p.m.	61183	—	41A	C853	Blackburn
12.22	61316	—	41A	C854	Blackburn

Depot Coding: **15E** - Leicester (Cen); **41A** - Sheffield (Darnall); **50A** - York; **84A** - Wolverhampton (Stafford Rd); **84F** - Stourbridge Jct; **84G** - Shrewsbury.

The 1960 FA Cup Final was between Wolverhampton Wanderers and Blackburn, an excellent combination to ensure a healthy number of special workings from both Wolverhampton and Blackburn down the GW&GC Joint through Denham. On this occasion I chose Denham Golf Club to view the specials which are documented in the table opposite. 6022 KING EDWARD III rattles a Wolves special working No.22 through Denham Golf Club. The football team colours streamed from the windows leaving no doubt regarding the origination of the special.

I returned to the same location in 1961 to view the procession of football specials on Cup Final day. This time I photographed a Sheffield Darnall "B1" 61169, with a train from Leicester. The engine requires no effort to tackle the down grade through the Golf Club station. This was the fast stretch for the "Kings" on expresses from Birkenhead before the line was reclassified to secondary importance upon electrification of the London Midland West Coast route and closure of Birmingham (Snow Hill) station.

TABLE 41. **Tuesday Afternoon at SEER GREEN AND JORDANS - 20th April 1965.** Traffic flow 2.50 p.m. to 4.50 p.m.

Time	Loco. No.	Name	Direction	Train Description
2.55	45301	—	Up	Parcels
2.59	d.m.u.	—	Down	Suburban
3.23	d.m.u.	—	Up	Suburban
3.34	D1609	—	Down	Paddington to Shrewsbury
3.43	D5090	—	Down	Goods
3.49	D1709	—	Up	*CAMBRIAN COAST EXPRESS*
3.59	d.m.u.	—	Down	Suburban
4.17	d.m.u.	—	Down	Suburban
4.23	D1002	WESTERN EXPLORER	Down	Unidentified Express (Relief)
4.24	d.m.u.	—	Up	Suburban
4.35	D1685	—	Down	Paddington to Birkenhead
4.41	D1036	WESTERN EMPORER	Up	Birkenhead to Paddington
4.50	7908	HENSHALL HALL	Down	Paddington to Banbury

Ashendon Junction to the Great Central main line and the inevitable singling of the track between Princes Risborough and Banbury, following rationalisation programmes.

In the 1950's the Western Region were fond of running Sunday excursions to Wolverhampton using the direct line from Paddington to Birkenhead. I remember the fare being 18/6d, which was very reasonable at the time. It is difficult to believe the excursion journeys that could be made for less than £1 in those now far off days of everyday steam travel. It was inevitable that such opportunities could not be missed, particularly when the added attraction of securing 'visitor' permits for Wolverhampton locomotive works, Stafford Road and Oxley engine sheds made the trips even more worthwhile.

Towards the closing days of steam, when "Western" and "Brush" type 4 diesels were used on most main line workings to and from Paddington, I ventured further north to Wellington and Shrewsbury where a feast of steam was still to be enjoyed. A sojourn at Wellington (Salop) was particularly enjoyable since the locomotive shed was situated adjacent to the island platform enabling the comings and goings to be observed. The shed had no turntable and was the home of a small number of tank engines, although an occasional tender engine paid the coaling stage a visit.

Nowhere on the Paddington to Birkenhead line was the fringe of Western Region territory more evident than north of Wellington. A liberal helping of Midland Region engines spiced the traffic flow with "Black 5's", "8F's", "Jubilees" and various Midland Region tanks. One particular WR engine, 7817 GARSINGTON MANOR, seemed to follow me on my travels. Despite being reallocated from Croes Newydd to Reading it turned up carrying a Reading shed plate whilst on a freight during a spell of observation at Wellington station on 18th April 1964. A visit to Wellington was actually a staging post on a journey to Shrewsbury, as were Birmingham (Snow Hill) and Wolverhampton (Low Level) stations. Although stopping off at Birmingham, Wolverhampton and Wellington left little time at Shrewsbury before the return trip to Paddington.

The attraction of travelling as far north as Shrewsbury was to see "Manors" working their usual turns, across Wales to Aberystwyth. The site of so many Midland Region engines was something of a bonus.

The driver oils the motion of "Modified Hall" 7905 FOWEY HALL at Banbury shed in preparation to relieve D1011 WESTERN THUNDERER, which was running very late with the 2.10 p.m. from Paddington to Birkenhead on 9th June 1963. The camera position for this picture had to be very carefully chosen so that the smoke from the chimney obscured the telegraph post. To the rear of the tender the locomotive shed can be seen with at least two 9F's prominent.

(above) D1011 WESTERN THUNDERER crawls into Banbury past the locomotive shed having presumably suffered partial failure. The subject of the previous photograph, 7905 FOWEY HALL had already left the depot to relieve D1011 at the station.

(opposite) Another Cup Final day - 2nd May 1964, and West Ruislip was the vantage point chosen to view the Wembley specials. Preston were in the final and the Saturday morning of Cup Final day would be busy with extra traffic. In this scene special working 1X77 was photographed on the up centre track through West Ruislip station with Brush Type 4 D1717 in charge. In the siding beyond the bridge is D5514 with a rake of empty stock which had previously been occupied by football fans. Other specials observed on that day were hauled by "Black 5's" 44684 and 44765 together with "Britannia's" 70000 BRITANNIA, 70050 FIRTH OF CLYDE and 70052 FIRTH OF TAY.

A "Manor" was almost a certainty on the prestigious *CAMBRIAN COAST EXPRESS* which traversed the Cambrian lines to Aberystwyth and Pwllheli. The "Manor" was frequently a Machynlleth engine, which was expertly turned out by staff at its home depot. I remember that in 1964 Machynlleth "Manors" had white painted buffers and smoke box door hinges which identified these Welsh engines at some distance from the observer. The scarcity of "Manors" in my home based London division ensured that the last Western named engine remaining unseen on my travels was inevitably a member of this class - 7828 ODNEY MANOR. This, the penultimate class member, was indeed a rarely seen machine outside its home territory.

I had seen all named locomotives of Western origin with the exception of 7828 at least twice, some many hundreds of times. In August 1961, 7828 was operating from Croes Newydd shed (84J), in Wrexham, and the opportunity to see her came on 27th August; by official arrangement no less! Somewhat reminiscent of the old railway gentleman in the book 'The Railway Children', a retired railway official with connections in the right places managed to establish the most likely time at which ODNEY MANOR would be on Croes Newydd shed: 8.00 a.m. Sunday August 27th.

In the dead of night we set off in his trusted green Hillman Minx in search of this elusive engine. The only encumbrance being a small bag with notebook, pencil and a number of sandwiches. I remember it was 5 o'clock on that August Sunday morning when we arrived at the depot, three hours ahead of schedule. We decided to wait until 5.30 a.m., during which time breakfast consisted of sandwich remainders and semi-cold tea.

Having registered an early arrival at the Foreman's office we were shown the entrance to the covered accommodation. There was no need to enquire if ODNEY MANOR was resident at that early hour of the morning, for she was placed in the most prominent position for immediate spotting. The satisfaction achieved by the shed staff was evident in their smiles as they mused over the length of journey we had made to see the pride of their allocation. ODNEY MANOR was the only named engine on shed among the forty inhabitants, most of which were tank engines used for freight and shunting duties.

I never saw 7828 again on BR metals after that morning, but no doubt she was used frequently by Croes Newydd between Shrewsbury and Chester and on the Ruabon to Dolgellau line. Later, memories of this engine came flooding back when I saw her looking very sorry for herself in the scrapyard at Barry Docks. Her boiler strapping was prised open allowing it to bounce in the strong, corrosive coastal winds that sweep across the dockland in winter. However I presume this apparent attack on the locomotives last remaining dignity was to check its condition for potential preservation. Needless to say I was very pleased when ODNEY MANOR took to the rails again after many years of hard preservation work.

The main objectives of the trip to Wrexham had been completed, but the Hillman and its occupants still had a long day to look forward to as we worked out way south via Wellington locomotive depot (84H), a brief stop at Bromsgrove station and finally a visit to Banbury shed (84C).

Notable at Wellington was Gloucester Barnwood's sole Stanier 0-4-4T, 41900, lying dead at the rear of the shed. There were only fifteen engines on shed (a full house) of which ten were Panniers. A brief stop at Bromsgrove station produced "9400" Pannier's 8401 and 8403 together with "9F" 92079, all used for Lickey incline banking duties. Sunday on Banbury shed was very quiet with most of the engines gently simmering and little sign of any impending action. "9F's" and "WD" 2-8-0's were waiting patiently for Monday morning and a return to their heavy freight duties. The full list of the locomotives observed at Croes Newydd, Wellington and Banbury are shown in *Tables 42 - 44*.

It is sad to reflect on the fate of the line from Paddington to Shrewsbury, now reduced to secondary status with closed stations, severed sections and much reduced services. Only photographic images and the written word bring back memories of the engine sheds and the locomotives of the line resting in railway history.

TABLE 42 **CROES NEWYDD (84J) Motive Power Depot 5.30 a.m. 27th August 1961.**

1600 Cl.	1618; 1619; 1660.
2251 Cl.	2201; 2236.
2800 Cl.	3815; 3846.
4300 Cl.	6306; 6336; 7310; 7314.
5101 Cl.	4155.
5600 Cl.	5651; 6610; 6611; 6615; 6617; 6632; 6674; 6694; 6698.
5700 Cl.	3630; 3689; 3749; 3760; 4617; 5774; 8727; 8734; 9669; 9793.
7200 Cl.	7213; 7228.
7400 Cl.	7409; 7414; 7431; 7442; 7443.
7800 Cl.	7828 ODNEY MANOR.
Cl. 2MT	46513.

Total: 40.

TABLE 43 **WELLINGTON (84H) Motive Power Depot - 27th August 1961.**

5700 Cl.	3607; 3619; 3626; 3732; 3744; 4605; 9630; 9636; 9639; 9774.
Cl. 2MT	41201; 41204; 41231; 41241.
Cl. 2P	41900.

Total: 15.

TABLE 44 **BANBURY (84C) Motive Power Depot - 27th August 1961.**

1000 Cl.	1000 COUNTY OF MIDDLESEX.
2800 Cl.	2859.
4300 Cl.	6317; 7327.
4900 Cl.	4918 DARTINGTON HALL; 5945 LECKHAMPTON HALL; 5958 KNOLTON HALL; 6906 CHICHELEY HALL; 6923 CROXTETH HALL; 6925 HACKNESS HALL; 6929 WHORLTON HALL; 6952 KIMBERLEY HALL.
5101 Cl.	4149; 4152; 4154.
6400 Cl.	6421.
6800 Cl.	6856 STOWE GRANGE; 6861 CRYNANT GRANGE.
6959 Cl.	6964 THORNBRIDGE HALL; 6983 OTTERINGTON HALL; 7905 FOWEY HALL; 7929 WYKE HALL.
Cl. 8F	48431.
Cl. 5MT	73012.
Cl. WD	90148; 90268; 90315; 90691; 90693.
Cl. 9F	92207; 92214; 92227; 92236.

Total : 33 Steam plus 4 unrecorded diesel shunters = 37

(opposite) **At the rear of Banbury shed on 9th June 1963 stand "2800" 3845 and "2251" 2289. Banbury shed closed in October 1966, but already by 1963 the shed surroundings were looking decidedly run down with piles of rubble and tangles of wire littering the ground.**

TABLE 45.
Run - Paddington to Banbury
Train - **9.10 a.m. Paddington - Birkenhead**.
Date: **18th April 1964**.
Locomotive: Co-Co Type 4 (Cl.47) **D1682**.
Load: circa 416 Tons Tare, circa 440 Tons Gross.

Distance	Location	Actual min. sec.	Speeds m.p.h.
0	Paddington	00 00	-
1¼	Westbourne Park	03 55	27 (sigs)
3¼	Old Oak	07 20	-
7¾	Greenford	11 45	78
10	Northolt	13 30	82
12	West Ruislip	14 53	86/88
14¾	Denham	16 48	85
15¾	Denham Golf Club	17 25	83
17½	Gerrards Cross	18 42	82
20¼	Seer Green & Jordans	20 40	83
21¾	Beaconsfield	21 49	82
26½	High Wycombe arr.	26 36	-
	High Wycombe dep.	30 22	-
31½	Saunderton	37 15	63/65
34¾	Princes Risborough	40 14	62
37½	Ilmer	42 24	87/88
40	Haddenham	44 17	83
44	Ashendon Junction	47 04	88
47½	Brill	49 29	86/88
50½	Blackthorn	51 25	86/88
53½	Bicester North	53 25	86
57¼	Ardley	56 17	83/85
62½	Aynho	60 43	58/62
64	Kings Sutton	62 10	72/80
67½	Banbury Arr.	65 31	-

Average Speed: 61.8 m.p.h.

TABLE 46.
Run - Banbury to Paddington
Train - **2.45 p.m. Birkenhead - Paddington**.
Date: **18th April 1964**.
Locomotive: Co-Co Type 4 (Cl.47). **D1710**.
Load: circa 416 Tons Tare, circa 440 Tons Gross.

Distance	Location	Actual min. sec.	Speeds m.p.h.
0	Banbury	00 00	-
3½	Kings Sutton	05 13	65
5	Aynho	06 41	71
10¼	Ardley	11 19	64/78
14	Bicester North arr	26 01	-
-	Bicester North dep	17 33	-
17	Blackthorn	21 54	63
20	Brill	25 33	70/66/76
23½	Ashendon Junction	27 42	54
27½	Haddenham	31 12	72/75
30	Ilmer	33 24	71
32¾	Princes Risborough	35 48	65
36	Saunderton	38 48	59/74
41	High Wycombe arr	45 12	-
-	High Wycombe dep	47 01	-
45¾	Beaconsfield	54 38	60
47¼	Seer Green & Jordans	56 05	70
50	Gerrards Cross	58 12	82
51¾	Denham Golf	59 24	90
52¾	Denham	60 00	92/94
55½	West Ruislip	61 48	88
57½	Northolt	63 15	86
59	Greenford	64 44	92
62¾	Park Royal	66 49	83
66¼	Westbourne Park	70 50	30
67½	Paddington	73 45	-

Average Speed : 54.9 m.p.h

(above) **"5700" Pannier 9753 trundles a transfer freight through Birmingham (Snow Hill) on 22nd September 1962. This class was the most numerous on the Great Western system, totalling 863 locomotives, a worthy tribute to their designer C.B. Collett. The significance of the chalked '1' on the side tank is not clear, but may have represented the roster for this locomotive on the day.**

(left) **5089 WESTMINSTER ABBEY, bereft of a shed plate and looking decidedly filthy, poses for a photograph at Wolverhampton (Low Level) on 18th April 1964. This engine was one of twelve "Castles" converted from "Stars". Note the trolleybus wires over the road bridge, but the vehicle on the bridge has no current collection gear and must therefore be a humble motor bus.**

(opposite, bottom) **My notes, dated 18/4/64, recorded this as the 3.42 p.m. arrival from Aberystwyth. The short train is hauled by Std. 2-6-4T 80079 which was allocated to Croes Newydd. Somehow I cannot imagine how this service could have been economical. This particular engine has secured a new lease of life in preservation on the Severn Valley Railway.**

During my visit to Wellington on 18th April 1964 I had not expected to see 7817 GARSINGTON MANOR, then allocated to Reading, heading south with a freight train. Before transfer to Reading this engine would have been quite at home on this stretch of track being allocated to Croes Newydd.

This scene, facing west at Basingstoke on 8th September 1962, is one of my favourite photographs, taken before my photography had attained its present day capability. "West Country" 34104 BERE ALSTON heads a Waterloo-Bournemouth express. On the adjacent track, held at the signals, Standard class "4" 75077 is in charge of an empty stock working.

10: DAYS ON THE SOUTHERN

My first experience of travels on the Southern were from Charing Cross to Chelsfield in an electric multiple unit during the 1950's. Although the e.m.u's of the time did not capture my interest, the "Schools" class 4-4-0's certainly did. These superb machines were the motive power for the Hastings and Deal expresses via Sevenoaks and Tonbridge. During my various visits to Southern metals I managed to see all 40 members of the class. The most elusive being 30915 BRIGHTON, the reason, I believe was the locomotive's allocation to Stewarts Lane which did not supply locomotives for the Charing Cross services. Finally I managed to join a group visit to Stewarts Lane and was fortunate enough to catch the engine 'on shed'.

I enjoyed my visits to Chelsfield, which were basically arranged for the benefit of my grandmother, but a lot of my time was spent by the railway line! Most vivid in my recollection were the unrebuilt "Battle of Britain" engines slipping on wet rails on the climb from Orpington to Chelsfield; a first siting of "Britannia" 70014 IRON DUKE on the up line, with a Victoria bound *GOLDEN ARROW*, and two "Merchant Navy's", 35027 PORT LINE and 35028 CLAN LINE, both now preserved albeit in rebuilt form. These were, of course, in addition to the regular "Schools" turns rattling through the station.

Strangely, freight trains were totally absent from this line during my daytime visits, although I did see a permanent way train hauled by a 'C' class, the number of which was unrecorded in my notes. I must assume that passenger services on the line did not allow 'pathing' for goods trains and consequently must have run at night or taken alternative routes. My thoughts turned to why the railway needed Hither Green locomotive depot, the existence of the Kent coalfield and the inevitable goods traffic between Britain and the continent; all of which should have resulted in movement of freight. One of these days I will acquire a working timetable of the period and establish, out of interest, the pattern of freight workings in the area.

On a number of occasions, instead of Chelsfield station, I ventured onto the Victoria - Margate line through St. Mary Cray. Here a number of trains were hauled by "King Arthurs" with such majestic names as SIR CADOR OF CORNWALL, or SIR URRE OF THE MOUNT and the more humble SIR BRIAN.

All of these visits took place before my parents could afford to purchase a camera any better than a simple box brownie, which of course was of little use for movement photography. By the time I was the proud owner of more suitable photographic equipment my grandmother had passed away and the need to travel to Kent was over.

The nearest lineside spot to view Southern steam, from my home in Iver, was Egham. This was relatively close but a trip down the Staines branch from West Drayton to Staines (West) was necessary, having travelled from Iver to West Drayton by a Paddington bound suburban.

The Staines branch passenger services in the 1950's were often operated by Southall based diesel railcars. The later batch of railcars were sharp featured creatures in comparison to the smoother lines of the earlier models.

West Drayton was the junction for both the Uxbridge (Vine Street) and Staines (West) branches. Passenger services ceased on the Uxbridge branch in September 1962 and on the Staines branch in March 1965. In 1958 there were five stations on the latter branch inclusive of Staines (West), three of which were Halts, with Colnbrook as the principal intermediate station on the line. The site of Colnbrook can be found east of the village where the line crossed the Old Bath Road.

My journey to Staines (West) was during the final summer of operation of the railcars and auto-trains on the branch; they were replaced by diesel multiple units in October of the same year. I did

This was one of my favourite haunts on the Waterloo main line to the South West. The location was west of Weybridge station and the vantage point a bridge used as a footpath which was well away from traffic noise and hazard. The bridge overlooked the junction for the Chertsey line, gave a fine view of the station in the eastwards direction and in this scene looking west, an excellent vista of the practically straight run into Byfleet and New Haw. The locomotive is rebuilt "Merchant Navy" 35019 FRENCH LINE CGT, with an up express from, I think, Southampton. Photographed 2nd August 1965.

TABLE 47. BYFLEET AND NEW HAW - 9TH AUGUST 1963. Traffic flow 2.30 p.m. to 6.30 p.m.

Time	Loco.	Name	Shed	Direction	Train Description
2.35	30506	—	70B	Up	Freight
2.36	E.M.U.	—		Down	Suburban
2.36	E.M.U.	—		Down	Waterloo to Portsmouth
2.37	E.M.U.	—		Up	Portsmouth to Waterloo
2.44	E.M.U.	—		Up	Suburban
2.55	34088	213 SQUADRON	70A	Down	Waterloo to Bournemouth
3.01	E.M.U.	—		Down	Suburban
3.02	30508	—	70B	Up	Light engine
3.05	34059	SIR ARCHIBALD SINCLAIR	70E	Up	Salisbury to Waterloo
3.12	E.M.U.	—		Down	Waterloo to Portsmouth
3.14	E.M.U.	—		Up	Suburban
3.24	73117	VIVIEN	70A	Up	Empty stock
3.25	35020	BIBBY LINE	70A	Down	Waterloo to Ilfracombe
3.27	35009	SHAW SAVILL	72A	Up	*ATLANTIC COAST EXPRESS*
3.28	34092	CITY OF WELLS	70E	Down	Waterloo to Basingstoke
3.30	E.M.U.	—		Down	Suburban
3.33	31617	—	70A	Up	Freight
3.34	E.M.U.	—		Up	Portsmouth to Waterloo
3.42	E.M.U.	—		Up	Suburban
3.44	35001	CHANNEL PACKET	70A	Up	Bournemouth to Waterloo
3.47	D6533	—	71A	Up	Parcels
3.51	D6527	—	73C	Down	Freight
3.54	34046	BRAUNTON	71B	Down	Waterloo to Bournemouth
3.57	34004	YEOVIL	71A	Down	Waterloo to Bournemouth
4.01	E.M.U.	—		Down	Suburban
4.02	E.M.U.	—		Up	Suburban
4.09	E.M.U.	—		Up	Suburban
4.09	E.M.U.	—		Down	Waterloo to Portsmouth
4.17	E.M.U.	—		Up	Empty stock
4.19	73115	KING PELINORE	70A	Down	Waterloo to Basingstoke
4.19	34034	HONITON	71A	Up	Bournemouth to Waterloo
4.30	E.M.U.	—		Down	Suburban
4.33	E.M.U.	—		Up	Portsmouth to Waterloo
4.35	E.M.U.	—		Up	Suburban
4.35	34058	SIR FREDERICK PILE	72A	Down	Milk empties
4.37	34037	CLOVELLY	71B	Up	Bournemouth to Waterloo
4.43	E.M.U.	—		Up	Portsmouth to Waterloo
5.06	34003	PLYMOUTH	70E	Up	Salisbury to Waterloo
5.16	E.M.U.	—		Up	Portsmouth to Waterloo
5.22	E.M.U.	—		Down	Waterloo to Portsmouth
5.22	E.M.U.	—		Up	Suburban
5.23	E.M.U.	—		Up	Portsmouth to Waterloo
5.27	D6537	—	73C	Down	Light engine
5.31	E.M.U.	—		Up	Farnham to Waterloo
5.37	E.M.U.	—		Up	Portsmouth to Waterloo
5.41	E.M.U.	—		Up	Portsmouth to Waterloo
5.44	34016	BODMIN	71A	Up	Southampton to Waterloo
5.47	E.M.U.	—		Down	Waterloo to Portsmouth?
5.58	73082	CAMELOT	70A	Up	Bournemouth to Waterloo
6.00	E.M.U.	—		Down	Waterloo to Portsmouth
6.01	E.M.U.	—		Down	Waterloo to Portsmouth
6.02	34094	MORTEHOE	70A	Up	Basingstoke to Waterloo
6.14	35006	PENINSULAR AND ORIENTAL S.N.CO.	70E	Up	Plymouth to Waterloo
6.16	E.M.U.	—		Up	Portsmouth to Waterloo
6.20	E.M.U.	—		Down	Suburban
6.21	34085	501 SQUADRON	71B	Up	*BOURNEMOUTH BELLE*
6.23	92231	—	71A	Up	Freight
6.28	E.M.U.	—		Down	Suburban
6.29	34097	HOLSWORTHY	71A	Up	Salisbury to Waterloo
6.29	34025	WHIMPLE	71A	Down	*ROYAL WESSEX*

Notes (1) During the afternoon a cable fire disrupted services, and in consequence train identification became difficult. The train descriptions are, therefore, as accurate as the circumstances allowed.

(2) Depot allocations were taken from the locomotives in passing, with some exceptions based upon allocations of January, 1963.

Depot Coding: **70A** - Nine Elms; **70B** - Feltham; **70E** - Salisbury; **71A** - Eastleigh; **71B** - Bournemouth; **72A** - Exmouth Jct; **73C** - Hither Green.

A down West of England line train stops at Basingstoke on 8th September 1962 with "Battle of Britain" 34051 WINSTON CHURCHILL in charge. The two reporting numbers on the smokebox door confuse train identification, but I believe 446 to be correct since chalked above the reporting number is 2.54 which may represent the departure time from Waterloo. I knew the unrebuilt Bullied Pacifics by the nickname "Spam Cans". On reflection this was unfair as I confess to be quite fond of the design.

not realise this would be the case at the time so, upon reflection, this was a timely trip in a railcar and the only one I was to experience. Having alighted at Staines (West), a relatively short walk was necessary from the WR station to my chosen location, a pedestrian overbridge adjacent to a level crossing between Staines S.R. and Egham stations.

Although there were regular interval electric multiple unit services on the branch, the interest lay in the freight services which were timed between the electrics, although not in every capacity gap. The freight used this line to gain access to Feltham Yard from the Southern main line, having diverged at Byfleet and New Haw and from the Western main line at Reading. A good mornings observations would include "S15's", "King Arthurs", "Q1's", "H16" Pacific tanks and Class "700" 0-6-0's.

After 1962, the numbers of ex-GWR locomotives were rapidly diminishing and in consequence reports of a continuing heavy usage of steam on the main line out of Waterloo drew my attention. This resulted in visits to Weybridge, Byfleet & New Haw and West Byfleet. This was an Indian Summer of steam with all the expresses to Bournemouth, Exeter and the Devon resorts being steam hauled. Further to this most of the freight was steam with the exception of an occasional D6500 diesel.

By 1965 there was still a preponderance of steam, but the Exeter trains were now the domain of "Warship" diesel hydraulics, which was not too disappointing; they were engines from the Western Region, where my original railway interest began back in 1953.

Table 47 records the traffic through Byfleet & New Haw on 9th August 1963. During the afternoon of that day, a cable fire on the line disrupted services, which caused some difficulty in train identification, causing much late running, so forgive me if an error can be identified in the descriptions. Steam traction on this line was still very much in evidence in 1966 resulting in the choice of rebuilt "Merchant Navy" 35030 ELDER DEMPSTER LINES as motive power for a Great Central railtour on the line's last day of operation as a through route on 3rd September.

The most unusual locomotive I observed on the Southern main line was former LNER "A4" Pacific MALLARD, running light through Byfleet presumably to take up an excursion commencing on Southern metals.

Further west, Basingstoke drew my attention for two reasons: access was straightforward via Reading and secondly the change of locomotives from Western to Southern types on the cross country turns on summer Saturdays. A wide variety of locomotive types were possible at Basingstoke: Great Western "Halls" and "Granges" and LM "Black 5's" were not uncommon. These were merely spice amidst the large number of Southern engines using the station.

The 1960s were not best remembered for the spate of branch line closures taking place all over the country. The 2nd November 1963 was the last day for services on the Hayling Island branch, so I could not miss the opportunity to see and travel behind a "Terrier" between Havant and Hayling Island.

The principal engine for the day was 32650, the activity of which I also recorded on 8mm colour film. Two other engines joined 32650 during the afternoon Nos: 32662 and 32670. These diminutive tanks were dwarfed by the carriages that they were hauling. If it was not for the profuse amount of steam these little engines generated one could be forgiven for believing the train to be self propelled when viewed from the rear.

Another photograph at Weybridge shows the final member of the BR Standard 2-6-4T class, 80154, chuffing up the relief line with a parcels train. The photograph was taken 2nd August 1965 and shows the over bridge from which the preceding main line photographs were taken.

After that final day of services, 32650 was placed in store at Eastleigh having covered over 1Zᴠ million miles. During its career, the little 0-6-0T enjoyed a six year spell on the Isle of Wight between May 1930 and May 1936. She is now preserved on the Kent & East Sussex Railway as No.10 SUTTON.

In all, eight "Terriers" saw service on the Isle of Wight but the motive power in the later years of steam on the Island were exclusively Class "02" 0-4-4 Tanks, which were the objective of visits made to the Island before steam ended.

Despite the uniformity of locomotive types on the Island there was nevertheless a magnetic attraction, since it was unusual for standard gauge tank engines to carry names in the later days of steam traction and this, coupled with the rather antique coaching stock used on the Island, created a railway atmosphere that could well have represented a much earlier era of railway history.

The centre of railway activity was the railhead at Ryde Pier and the locomotive shed and works at Ryde St. Johns. It was here that I journeyed shortly before the demise of steam on the Island.

My chosen film media on this final visit was 35mm colour slide and 8mm cine material. Unfortunately the cine film was mislaid by the processor, a much lamented loss. Simultaneously my companions 35mm slide film also suffered the same fate. A rather suspicious coincidence!

However, the memories remain of the "02" tanks with names such as SEAVIEW, FRESHWATER and CHALE. On that day there was a shortage of operational locomotives to maintain the services due to the running down of the fleet and the consequent 'less than pristine' condition of the locomotive stock. Happily one of the locomotives has been preserved, 24 CALBOURNE, which is now resident at Haven Street on the island's own preserved railway. It is surprising that a ready made model locomotive of an Isle of Wight "02" has not been produced but perhaps this comment will encourage

the production of one with an option of a variety of names. I can guarantee at least one prospective owner!

I have previously mentioned the Southern line from Reading (South) to Guildford, Tonbridge and the Kent coast. On the 19th August 1961, this line attracted me to observe the summer holiday traffic emanating from the West Midlands to the holiday resorts on the Kent coast and of course the return traffic which was equally of interest.

Crowthorne was chosen since the goods yard presented a suitable lineside observation point and a vantage position to take photographs with my folding and rather primitive, 2Zᴠ" square format, camera. This was not normally a busy line, but between 12 noon and 2.00 p.m. on a summer Saturday in 1961 it came briefly to life with holiday trains filling the gaps between the normal Reading to Redhill stopping trains. Western and Southern engines shared the honours which enabled Western "Moguls" and "Manors" to reach Redhill.

(opposite, bottom) **Without doubt the best loved tank engines on the Southern were the diminutive "Terriers". They were the mainstay of the Hayling Island branch service from Havant until the closure of the line from 3rd November 1963. On the last day of services, 32650 fills up with water at the buffer stops of the Hayling Island bay in Havant station.**

There's a little bit of magic about this picture, which I cannot explain. Obscure the British Railways logo on the side tank of the locomotive and the scene is timeless. This was the first Southern steam engine exposed in my cheap 2¼" square folding camera. Taken in the summer of 1960, the same scene could easily have been photographed twenty years earlier. The locomotive is "02" tank no.17 SEAVIEW. Details on the photograph emerge when studying the picture to provide its caption. In this case a plate over the buffer beam registers the rosta of the locomotive as number 9. Note the Isle of White ferry returning to the mainland and, perched on the railings, two seagulls shortly to be alarmed into flight.

(*above*) **I have included a number of pictures taken during the final day of operation on the Hayling Island branch simply because it was one of my fondest steam railway memories. This photograph shows 32650, returning from Hayling Island, making a scheduled stop at Langstone station.**

(*left*) **Later in the afternoon on the final day of Hayling Island services two other Terriers, 32662 and 32670, joined 32650 for the sad farewell. In this scene, on the island, 32670 takes a brim full load of passengers to the terminus at Hayling. It is ironical to speculate that if the train had been regularly loaded to the level experienced on its final day finance to upkeep the line and continue its operation may well have been possible.**